For Heath Miller and Gail Simone

PRAISE FOR CATHERYNNE M. VALENTE

"If most fantasy and Y.A. novels are like the breakfast cereals that kids sift in search of marshmallows and clusters of fruit, Valente's novels are all marshmallows and clusters." —*THE NEW YORKER*

PRAISE FOR THE FAIRYLAND SERIES

"One of the most extraordinary works of fantasy, for adults or children, published so far this century."

—**LEV GROSSMAN**, author of The Magicians series, for *Time* magazine

"A glorious balancing act between modernism and the Victorian Fairy Tale, done with heart and wisdom."

—**NEIL GAIMAN**, Newbery Award-winning author of *The Graveyard Book* and *American Gods*

"September is a clever, fun, stronghearted addition to the ranks of bold, adventurous girls. Valente's subversive storytelling is sheer magic."

—**TAMORA PIERCE**, author of The Immortals series

"A mad, toothsome romp of a fairy tale—full of oddments, whimsy, and joy."

—**HOLLY BLACK**, author of *Doll Bones* and *The Cruel Prince*

"When I saw that this book reminds me simultaneously of E. Nesbit, James Thurber, and the late Eva Ibbotson, I don't mean to take anything away from its astonishing originality. It's a charmer from the first page, managing the remarkable parlay of being at once ridiculously funny and surprisingly suspenseful. Catherynne Valente is a find, at any age!"

—**PETER S. BEAGLE**, author of *The Last Unicorn*

Also by CATHERYNNE M. VALENTE

SPACE OPERA

THE GLASS TOWN GAME

SIX-GUN SNOW WHITE

THE REFRIGERATOR MONOLOGUES

CATHERYNNE M. VALENTE

With illustrations by Annie Wu

SAGA PRESS

1230 AVENUE OF THE AMERICAS, NEW YORK, NEW YORK 10020

This book is a work of fiction. Any references to historical events, real people, or real places are used fictitiously. Other names, characters, places, and events are products of the author's imagination, and any resemblance to actual events or places or persons, living or dead, is entirely coincidental.

For information about special discounts for bulk purchases, please contact Simon & Schuster Special Sales at 1-866-506-1949 or business@simonandschuster.com.
The Simon & Schuster Speakers Bureau can bring authors to your live event. For more information or to book an event, contact the Simon & Schuster Speakers Bureau at 1-866-248-3049 or visit our website at www.simonspeakers.com.
Also available in a Saga Press hardcover edition
The text for this book was set in Electra.
The illustrations for this book were rendered digitally.
Manufactured in the United States of America
First Saga Press paperback edition March 2018
2 4 6 8 10 9 7 5 3 1
Library of Congress Cataloging-in-Publication Data
Names: Valente, Catherynne M., 1979– author. | Wu, Annie, illustrator.
Title: The refrigerator monologues / Catherynne M. Valente ; with illustrations by Annie Wu.
Description: First edition. | London ; New York : Saga Press, an imprint of Simon & Schuster, Inc., [2017]
Identifiers: LCCN 2016040142 (print) | LCCN 2016047166 (eBook) | ISBN 9781481459341 (hardcover : alk. paper) | ISBN 9781481459358 (trade paper : alk. paper) | ISBN 9781481459365 (eBook)
Classification: LCC PS3622.A4258 A6 2017 (print) | LCC PS3622.A4258 (eBook) | DDC 813/.6—dc23
LC record available at https://lccn.loc.gov/2016040142

THE REFRIGERATOR MONOLOGUES

THE HELL HATH CLUB

I'm dead. The deadest girl in Deadtown.

It's been a while now. I'm comfortable with the word. You wouldn't believe how comfortable the dead can get. We don't tiptoe.

Dead. Dead. Dead. Flying Ace of the Corpse Corps. Stepping the light Deathtastic. I don't actually know what a doornail is, but we have a lot in common. Dying was the biggest thing that ever happened to me. I'm famous for it. If you know the name Paige Embry, you know that Paige Embry died. She died at night. She died stupidly. She died for no reason. She fell off a bridge like a suicide leap and nobody caught her. She dropped into the water, her spine snapped, and the last things she probably saw was those astonishing lights in the sky, the lights of Doctor Nocturne's infernal machine igniting every piece of metal in the city, turning skyscrapers into liquid purple fire while Kid Mercury punched the bad guy over and over again, maybe because he was grieving already, maybe because he loved fighting more than girls and it was his biggest fight yet, maybe because that's what the script of his life told him to do, maybe because he couldn't stop. Paige Embry died watching her boyfriend save New York City. When the fires went out in Manhattan, they went out in her eyes, too.

It's nice to be famous for something, I guess.

And the thing about me is, I'm not coming back. Lots of people do, you know. Deadtown has pretty shitty border control. If you know somebody on the outside, somebody who knows a guy, a priest or a wizard or a screenwriter or a guy whose superpower shtick gets *really* dark sometimes or a scientist with a totally neat revivification ray who just can't seem to get federal funding, you can go home again.

But we go steady, Death and me. Nobody can tear us apart.

Not everybody wants to go back. Life's okay in Deadtown. The early bird special lasts all day and the gas is free. There's no fiery rings of artisanal punishment down here. Just neighborhoods. Blackstones. Bodegas. Walk-up apartments with infinite floors. The subways run on time. Yeah, sure, there's skulls and femurs and gargoyles all over the place and the architects never met a shade of black they didn't like, but hey—good design is all about a unified aesthetic. You get used to it. It starts to feel like home. And the gargoyles are really nice guys. The one living on my balcony is called Brian. He has three heads and he's super into slam poetry. Deadtown is like anyplace else. It's scary at first, but you get into a rhythm. Find a favorite park. Put a couple of pictures up on your wall. Pretty soon, you can't imagine living anywhere else.

Not everyone adjusts. I've seen girls run down the main drag toward the EXIT sign with smiles on their faces that would break you in half. Then again, I've seen others dragged back to the land of the living, screaming and sobbing and clawing through the dirt till their fingernails snap off and their mouths fill up with snot.

But not me. No way. No how. If there's a constant in the universe, it's that Paige Embry is dead. I am a permanent error page. 404: Girl Not Found. Oh, sure, I know a guy on the outside. A pretty damn powerful guy. A guy with the speed of a maglev train, the brainpower of a supercomputer, and the strength of a half-dozen Hollywood Hercules. A guy who can slalom between skyscrapers like gravity forgot to take down his name and number. But he's never once peeked in on me. Never once caught me, in all the times I've fallen. I hear he's dating now. We do get the news here in Deadtown. Every morning in four colors. He's got somebody prettier than a lipstick ad who'll stay home while he fights crime, waving from a window in a goddamn apron. I bet *she* lives forever.

I think about Tom Thatcher a lot. Kid Mercury. I came up with that name, you know. He wanted to call himself Mr. Mercury. But I said, *Tommy, that sounds like a car dealership. You're eighteen. You're not even halfway to being a Mister yet. We're still kids, you and me.*

The thing I hate about being dead is you can't move on. I was in love with him when I died, so I'll be in love with him till the sun burns out. I used to say that actual thing, curled up next to Tom in bed, my leg draped over Kid Mercury's marvelous thigh, as romantic as a heart-shaped balloon.

I'll love you till the sun burns out.

Well, now it's factually, actually true and it is just a huge bummer. I'm frozen. I'm stuck. I'm Paige Embry forever, the Paige Embry that died with all that violet flame flickering in her blank eyes. I can never be anyone else. I can never see a therapist or eat all the ice cream ever made or go out with my friends and drunk-dial him and tell him I hate him and I never came when he fucked me, not even once, not even after he got his powers, and then call again in the morning and apologize and hide in my couch watching a million episodes of *Law & Order* all in a row. I don't get to start dating again. I get to wait in a black window for a guy who's never coming home.

At least it's a nice window.

But one thing the dead do love is telling our stories. We get to take our stories with us. They don't take up a lick of room in the suitcase. Most days I leave my apartment in Hell's Kitchen (actual Hell's actual Kitchen), go down to the Lethe Café, order a cup of nothing, look out the window at the blue-gas burntbone streetlamps, and wait for the girls. Ladies who lunch. Ladies who lost. You don't have to be lonely down here if you don't want to be. They come one by one, all big eyes and long legs, tucking strands of loose hair behind their ears, carrying pocketbooks and hats and secret griefs. Julia, Pauline, Daisy, Bayou, Samantha and more and others. Every time they open the frosted-glass door a gust of autumn leaves and moonlight blows in and sticks against the legs of the tables. They apologize to Neil, the gargoyle behind the espresso machine. He shakes his big woolly wolfshead, pulls a black *ristretto* shot of emptiness and says, *Don't you worry about it, honey*.

It's always autumn in Deadtown. It's always the middle of the night, even at nine in the morning.

We call ourselves the Hell Hath Club.

There's a lot of us. We're mostly very beautiful and very well-read and very angry. We have seen some shit. Our numbers change—a few more this week, a few less next, depending on if anyone gets called up to the big game. You can't keep your lunch date if some topside science jockey figures out how to make a zombie-you. We're totally understanding about that sort of thing. She'll be back. They always come back. Zombies never last, power sputters out, and clones don't have the self-preservation instinct God gave a toddler in a stove shop.

I watch them come and go and, sometimes, for a minute, I

think that sweet-faced geek in his lab will reanimate *my* rotting corpse for once. But he never looks twice at me. Never picked myself for the team for all eternity.

I guess you could call me the President of the Hell Hath Club. It's honorary and empty and mostly means I get to the café first and hold our table. I order for everyone. I keep the minutes, such as they are. And when the girls settle in, we open our stories up like the morning edition. News, sports, stocks, funny pages. It's all right there, neat and tidy and well-crafted and *finished*. Everything that ever happened to us. With a big fat D-Day headline over the part where magic became real, superheroes hit the scene, and the world went absolutely, unashamedly, giggles-and-lollipops-for-good-behavior crazy.

PAIGE EMBRY IS DEAD

Trouble is, my story is his story. The story of Kid Mercury crowds out everything else, like Christmas landing on the shops in August while Halloween tries to get a bat in edgewise. It's not his fault. I'm not even mad. Who wants to hear about an intern eking out a 2.21% improvement in the structural cohesion and tensile strength of an experimental alloy when they could look out the window of her *very* productive lab and see a guy in a slick silver suit swinging a haymaker at the metallic jaw of a former professor of music theory? BAM. POW. No contest. I have to try to squeeze in around the edges of him, to cram my little witch's hat on the department store shelf next to his great fat silver star.

Picture me as I was then. Paige Embry, pretty as a penny in a ponytail, turning up to Falk Industries every morning with what I used to cheerfully call my Cyanide Breakfast—a triple almond latte in my shiny, only slightly dented steel thermos. God *damn*, I used to love my lab coat! It made me feel invincible. A knight in shining polyester. I was gonna be twenty-two so fucking soon. I was gonna graduate with honors in overachieving-know-it-all studies. I was gonna throw my stupid mortarboard in the stupid air and it was gonna hang there for this long beautiful golden endless moment, like the last shot in a sitcom, before falling back into my arms filled up to the brim with tomorrows. The future looked so good on me.

Not bad for an invisible-class nobody. You know the invisible classes. They're the ones you never see till you need them. My dad was a garbageman. My mom was a night nurse. My whole childhood was made up of wee hours. Until I met Tom Thatcher, my favorite things in the world were C++, metallurgy, a shade of matte lipstick called the Grapes of Math, and Frosty Frogs cereal. Every single day of my life, I lived for the hour after my mother came home from the hospital, before my father started up his truck in the driveway, when the stars still held onto the sky by their fingertips and I sat at the kitchen counter, swinging my legs, eating my bowl of Frosty Frogs and listening to my parents be married to each other. You'd think Dad would have smelled horrific all the time, but he didn't. He smelled like coffee grounds, no matter how many times he showered.

"People throw out enough coffee in this city to keep the whole world awake till Judgment Day, Paigy. You should eat something besides that sugary crap, you know. Why don't you make her a soft-boiled egg, Nora? Brainiacs need protein or they keel over." And he'd whistle and spin woozily on his heel like a cartoon.

My mom sighed the same when I was seven as when I was seventeen. Her sigh was the prettiest part of her. Dad once said he knew it was love when he realized he'd jump off a cliff just to hear one exasperated sigh out of Nora Embry's mouth.

She's a vegetable now.

The Arachnochancellor wrapped my mother up in his Web of Illusion and left her there to starve and suffocate and even though Tom rescued the hell out of her she never woke up. It happens. What are you going to do? When the world loses its fucking mind and turns on you like a stupid feral cat you thought was tame, it happens. Everyone does the long, woozy whistle and keels over.

You get real honest when you're dead. So let me give it to you straight: it's my fault. Catatonic mom? My fault. Kid Mercury? My fault. The Arachnochancellor and Doctor Nocturne and those singing, boiling violet lights over Manhattan? They belong to me. I own them.

Not me alone, of course. I was only an intern. But it came from my lab. My *project*. What a fathomless world can live in the slim space of 2.21%.

It was such a nothing assignment. Busy work, really. Falk Industries loves the military-industrial complex like a kid in a blue tuxedo loves his date to the prom, and the military only ever wants two things from her suitors: new stuff that blows up or new stuff to keep other stuff from getting blown up. I was on Team No Blow Up. We were developing new alloys for use in body and vehicle armor—flexible, lightweight, strong, all those fun things that actually don't play together so nicely unless you start telling them who's boss on the molecular level. That was my job. Making metals and chemicals go out on charming little dates and drink charming little cocktails and make charming little astonishingly useful babies. It's all so totally toxic, you need your own body armor even to take most of our toys out of the box. We had a prototype. Liquid armor. Take one bath and you're good to work out your testosterone on unsuspecting nationalities for a solid diner shift of eight hours—if we could find a way to make it stop burning your skin off and eating through the floor of your infantry tank while smelling weirdly like baking cookies. I'd gotten us 2.21% closer to the promised land of nobody's flesh melting.

Who wouldn't sneak their boyfriend in at night to see a bulletproof bubble bath that smelled like oatmeal chocolate chip?

Tom and I met in class. Music theory. Dr. Alastair Augustus presiding. We'd both played piano since we were kids. Mom insisted that the upright Dad hauled back from some Upper East Side curb was only a little out of tune and besides I'd regret it if I woke up at fifty and had never learned an instrument. Tom's parents died when he was little, but his aunt felt similarly about the epidemic of modern children growing up with only enough knowledge to hit play on a glowing screen. Dr. Augustus was a wonderful lecturer. Tall and thin in his dark suits and floppy hair, gesturing wildly with his good hand. He'd lost the other in Kuwait. You'd think he wouldn't want to talk about it, but Dr. A wasn't like that. He'd tell you anything you wanted to know. He flapped around his lecture hall like a jazz crow stuck in the building with no way out, squawking: *Music theory is just math you can groove to.*

Tom and I are both front-row wave-your-hands-in-the-air-like-you-just-really-care-way-too-much types. One day, Dr. A asked us to stay after. He'd written a piece for five hands, and he wanted to take it for a spin. Tom's, mine, his. We sat at the bench with the professor behind us, dusty afternoon sun sneaking in through the high windows to pool in the empty chairs and listen. We made a mess of it at first. You can imagine. Frantic eyes jumping between the sheet music and our leaping tangle of fingers. But slowly, the melody sorted itself between us, beneath our hands, filling up the hall with a strange, frantic sorrow.

It was a nocturne.

By the time we'd finished, Tom and I were a couple, even though we hadn't said a word to each other. Music is an asshole like that.

I remember lying next to him in his childhood bedroom, which looked like someplace computers went to have nervous breakdowns and die. Motherboards and soldering irons and cables, oh my. Old *TRON* and *WarGames* posters on the wall next to that awful cheesecake shot of a be-sweatered and bespectacled Glenn Falk of Falk Industries lying across his desk in nineteen eighty whatever. I pulled up the sheet a little—it felt weird to have my CEO watch me fuck Tom Thatcher for the first time with that smug come-hither stare. But I was happy. The sex was sweet and deep and good. We made do with four hands. I'd stepped on an old keyboard at one point and snapped off the vowels and a good spray of consonants. Now, after, Tom snuggled against me, rolling the M key over his thumb and his forefinger. I looked up through the spaces between the bones of his hand at the moon outside the window. M is for lots of things. Moon. Midnight. Mine. Mercury. Pretty soon it would be the Frosty Frogs hour.

"You're like the boy version of me," I sighed.

"I think you'll find you're the girl version of me," Tom said, and whenever he said anything, there was a little laughter in it—not cruel laughter, just leftover crumbs of delight in the world and himself and human speech.

"I mean, obviously, my science is way cooler than your science, but I accept your lifestyle choices. You can fix my computer while I save the world."

Tom clutched invisible pearls. This is the mating dance of the lab scientist and the computer engineer. View our majestic plumage. "You bite your tongue! Cool is as cool does. And when those fancy Falk mainframes start horking up ASCII pictures of Sailor Moon instead of meekly processing your results, who you gonna call? That's right, your big, strong, super *cool* boyfriend to make it all better."

That's when everything changed. Right then. Watch it happen.

I sat up, not caring one bit if Glenn W. Falk III saw my tits, and said:

"You wanna see cool? Come with me. I'll show you cool."

The lab was quiet at four AM. Fluorescent lights and shadows and my brand-new 2.21% improved solution, the color of Frosty Frogs by moonlight. I've gone over it in my head a hundred times since. A thousand times. Because listen: Paige Embry practices Good Laboratory Hygiene. Perfect laboratory hygiene, in fact. I got into my hazmat suit and put Tom in Jimmy Keeler's. They were about the same size. I checked the seals twice. I inspected the fabric for any micro-tears, felt my ears pop as the seals locked in our helmets, and gave Tom the thumbs-up. Protocols: I follow them. I fucking *love* protocols. Protocols are a girl's best friend. So, I don't understand. I still don't understand.

"So, this is what you do," Tom said from beneath his plastic mask. "You do goop. All hail, Queen of Goop."

"Okay, it's not that impressive in its resting state." It really wasn't. We called it hypermercury, even though there wasn't much mercury in it anymore. It just sounded badass. At that moment, a couple of tablespoons of hypermercury sat at the bottom of my beaker like snot in fancy dress, doing absolutely nothing. "Hold out your hand."

Girls do dumb things to impress boys. I'm no different. But I swear it was safe. I'd done it on myself, on Jimmy Keeler, on a New England Patriots bobblehead, even on Mr. Falk himself when he toured R&D last Thanksgiving. Our suits keep it off you. They're designed specifically for working with hypermercury. Maybe I missed a micro-tear. Maybe the gloves were degraded from the day's testing. Maybe that 2.21% I was so proud of made hypermercury just that tiniest bit more corrosive, that tiniest bit *hungrier*. I poured my goop onto Tom Thatcher's fingertips—just a little. I swear, only a little.

At first, it did its thing and did it fabulously.

My happy silver mud flowed over his knuckles, mapping his hand, conforming, coating, encasing. Becoming a gauntlet that almost nothing could pierce or dent or scratch or penetrate in any fashion. Just like it was supposed to—better than it was supposed to. I could see the wrinkles of his glove forming in crisp, flawless silver. It was beautiful.

And then he started screaming.

Through the faceplate of his suit I could see Tom Thatcher's pretty face annihilate itself. Sudden thready veins snaked over his jaw—silver, white, blue, black—like frost cracking. Like dye falling through water. His eyes became hot diamonds, a million boiling crystal facets shredding his pupils. His stubble, the hair in his nose, his eyelashes, his eyebrows, all froze into steely icicles, then liquefied, sliding down over his cheeks, dripping, *weeping* off his chin. He said my name once.

Paige.

Then Tom fell down. When he got back up, everything in the world was different, and it would never go back.

He said *I'm okay* but he wasn't. He said *It didn't hurt* but it did. He said *I feel fine* but he lied.

He felt amazing.

Origin stories are like birthday parties: very exciting and colorful and noisy, but in the end, they're all the same. Anticipation sizzles around for weeks before the Big Day, but when it comes, your shindig looks pretty much like the one little Peter had last month.

There's an order of operations: take off your coats, pin the tail on the donkey, infection, singing, cake, mutation, balloons, gifts, branding, maybe a magician or a clown, exhaustion, and a bag of toys to take home. You're the same person today as yesterday. You just got a really big present and a shiny new hat to wear.

We stood outside the great glass doors of Falk Industries' midtown campus hip-deep in the last dregs of night and stars.

I saw it first.

Tom Thatcher, standing in a puddle of rain. But it wasn't rain. Too silvery, too thick, too opaque. It seeped from the soles of his feet, welled up, then bolted out ahead of him like a path through a fairy tale forest.

"Tom?" I asked. But he was already gone.

Tom vanished. That's what the speed of light looks like when you're standing still. He just tilted forward and disappeared, chasing the silver down 23rd Street, across the park, across the river, back to me, then up the side of the glassy Falk offices and over the top, leaping between skyscrapers like it was nothing, like he was hopping over Lego bricks he'd left on the floor of his room. I walked up to the N/R train subway entrance and waited for him to remember I existed. By the time he came silver-screaming down the stairwell, the sun had come up. Nothing can hide in the all-seeing light of dawn in Manhattan. Everything is just so totally clear.

"Holy shit," he said. "Did you see? Did you *see*?"

I did.

Back at his place, Tom and me went at it like fucking was an Olympic sport and we were after the gold.

Nobody ever talks about the sex. Nobody but the Hell Hath Club. I'll tell you something, it is unsettling as all hell. Tom turned into a hummingbird. So fast, touching every part of me at once, his fingertips crackling with the liquid lightning of hypermercury. With whatever hypermercury had become once it got inside him and unpacked all its secret belongings. Sometimes his eyes were diamonds. Sometimes they were human, brown and warm. Sometimes he was kissing me. Sometimes . . . sometimes *it* was. My work. My 2.21%. I could feel the difference on my lips. All the while, Glenn Falk III looked down from his poster, from his 1982 desk and his computer the size of a baby elephant.

Afterward, I lay there with one leg flung over his thigh, and we stated the obvious. Because it is *obvious*. I've seen a movie in my life. I've read a damn comic book. Why pretend there's some mystery to Hardy-Boy out? Dead rising from the grave? Eating brains? Only die with a headshot? You've got zombies, son. And when you come in contact with experimental goo and suddenly start leaping up the sides of buildings and punching through steel?

"So," Tom Thatcher said with a grin, "I'm clearly a superhero, right?"

"Clearly."

"Do I *have* to fight crime?" He whispered sweet everythings in my ear. "I mean, that's the classic career path. Computer science degree is to San Francisco start-up as superpower is to fighting crime. Never really wanted to be a cop, though."

I ran my fingers down the line of his jaw. "So don't be a cop. You don't *have* to do anything. Except maybe see a doctor? We can't be totally sure this is safe, it was nowhere near ready for human trials—"

Tom wasn't listening. "But I . . . I have a responsibility, don't I? To help people. If you're strong, you gotta use that strength. And I . . . I'm good, aren't I? I'm a good person. I could use it well. I could fix things. More than code. Debug the world, little bit by little bit. I can't just go back to school like nothing's different. You can't just shove power under the bed and expect it to stay put. It *wants* to be expressed. I just . . . I just have to do it carefully."

And that's why I went back to the lab and deleted my notes, my progress, everything leading to that strange, wily 2.21% improvement and everything coming from it. Because Tom Thatcher was a good person. I took the solution sample home with me. I didn't even break a sweat going through security. Turns out lying and stealing aren't that hard. If you've got a solid reason to sin, it's easy. It's nothing. This was my reason: one Kid Mercury was enough for the world. One good person could be trusted. Mass-produced Kid Mercuries could not.

Tom kissed me so fiercely that first morning. He could hardly contain himself. He started giggling and fell back on the bed.

"Oh my god, Paige, I *really* want a costume. Is that stupid? Can you sew?"

The garbageman's daughter could indeed sew.

Kid Mercury started slow. Entry-level stuff. Willing to work hard and learn, sir. Willing to work his way up. Purse snatchers and missing dogs, treed kittens and all that Sunday funny papers shit. We settled on silver and dark blue for the costume. Full body, mask and all. As aerodynamic as Francine's Fabric Depot and my wheezing dumpster-find Singer could manage. The first time he stopped a mugging, we went out for margaritas and sang karaoke in Koreatown till dawn. Tommy could do a surprisingly good boy-band croon. The first time he stopped a murder, we just walked out to the middle of the Brooklyn Bridge and stood there, looking at the stars and not saying anything—because what could you say? The traffic dopplered by behind us. We stared down into the water.

Three months later, I was going to die down there. In that filthy river. In the dark, in the light.

Dr. Augustus noticed Tom's good mood. Our tardiness. My distraction. He started following us. He was very good at it. I never saw. Tom never saw. When you're looking for muggers, you don't see the professor of music keeping watch two blocks behind. Dr. A had spent a long time overseas, learning to follow suspicious persons unseen through urban mazes. He never came at anything straight on.

"Come to dinner with me tonight, Paige," the professor said one day after the final. We both knew I'd aced it, despite everything. Back then, I could still be proud of a victory as small as an aced final. He slipped his good arm around my waist.

"I'm not sure that's completely appropriate, Dr. Augustus," I said, and laughed a little, opening the door for him to pretend it was a joke.

"Nonsense, my dear. My interest is *utterly* professional, I promise. And please, call me Alastair."

He picked me up at eight. Tom worried. We always worried about each other. For people as tightly wound as us, worry is love.

"It's weird. Don't you think it's weird? It's *pretty* weird," Kid Mercury fretted, the hood of his costume hanging down the back of his neck, his hair artfully mussed, the way I liked it.

"Have you ever met a pianist who isn't weird? Let alone a one-handed pianist who wears bow ties and has muttonchops. He probably just wants to get some free work-study hours out of me. Besides, you're hardly Captain Normal these days."

Kid Mercury gave me one of his perfect patented sidelong grins. "I *am* Captain Normal, thank you very much! Captain Normal of the Average Army, recipient of the Totally Regular Guy Medal of Honor."

I kissed him and pulled on my only really nice piece of clothing, a green velvet coat with real fox fur around the collar. My dad found it tossed on some glitterati trash bin. It only had a little stain on the fur and a few missing buttons. He'd fixed it up for Christmas for me. I stepped, in velvet and fur, out the door of Tom's apartment and into Dr. Augustus's car.

He bought me dinner first; I'll give him that. A golden French river of butter and garlic and game birds and champagne. We talked about his music. About my ambitions. About Tom. Quite a bit about Tom, really, but it's hard to see ominous patterns through champagne specs. After the crème brûlée, Alastair Augustus, PhD, opened the door of his long black sedan for me. I collapsed in a heap on the seat.

When he slid in beside me, he locked the doors.

I felt those locks click in my sternum, in the pit of my stomach. Every girl knows what that sound means. There's only a few choices left, once that vicious little church bell rings out. I still hear that sound over and over inside me, *click, click, click*.

"Where are we going?" I asked, fishing down into my gut for sobriety and coming up empty.

"Where else, Miss Embry? I'm taking you home. What sort of man do you think I am?"

No one would be home. It wasn't Frosty Frogs time yet. Mom would be at the hospital and Dad would be down at the depot, signing out his truck. I shrank against the seat. I wanted to be brave. I wanted to be clever. So I was. We stopped at a red light. I gulped air. In air is courage. I pulled my pocketknife out of my purse and jammed it in Dr. A's leg, then scrabbled at the lock, yanked it up, and stumbled out onto 6th Ave. But brave and clever isn't necessarily fast. I couldn't streak out over the city and run to New Jersey in forty-five seconds flat. Alastair Augustus whipped out his good hand and grabbed my hair in his fist. My hair and the fox-fur collar of Dad's Christmas coat. I hit my head on the roof of the car as he hauled me back in and leaned over to shut the door again.

"That's not how good girls behave, Paige," he said calmly, as though he'd caught me chewing gum in class. "And I know you *are* a good girl, so I expect you to act like one. Good girls want to *please*, Paige. Good girls do as they're told. And girls who are *very* good get sweets. Now, are you going to be a good girl for me?"

I kept my mouth shut, because what the fuck do you say to that? My head throbbed.

Dr. Augustus went on. His eyes looked so flat in the streetlights. "I'll tell you what else a good girl does. A good girl takes her gentleman friend into her house without any fuss. A good girl plays the hostess to a T. She brings out the *very best* for her guest. She goes to her nasty little hiding place and fetches whatever it is she gave to her moronic boyfriend to make him special. And she brings it out on a *silver tray*, Paige, because a good girl only gives up her treats to men who deserve it, *real* men, not skinny, sniveling weaklings who sit around on their computers all day. Do you understand, Paige? Are you a good girl?"

"No," I whispered. "I'm not." I didn't cry. Don't let anyone tell you I cried.

"Pity," sighed Alastair. "The world has run out of good girls. Whores like you are all that's left. But the nice thing about whores?" He leaned in. His breath smelled like the soft pale green after-dinner mints from the restaurant. "Whores give it up to everyone."

He came around to my side of the car and hauled me out by my hair, winding it around his knuckles. I felt the mouth of a gun against my back. Dr. Augustus shoved me through my own front door.

"Get me what I want, Paige. If you can't be a good girl, be a good dog. Fetch Daddy his slippers. Go on."

A voice came out of the shadows. "Did you two have a nice time? I hope you tipped the waitress."

Tom Thatcher, my Tom, Kid Mercury, leaned against the door of my bedroom, a hint of silver fabric showing under a soft black hoodie. I yelped in relief, an ugly, doglike sound. Tom glared at Dr. Augustus with diamond eyes. "They rely on tips, you know. They take care of you; you take care of them." A pool of quicksilver formed under his feet, angry and ready.

Alastair pulled his gun out of my spine so fast, I hardly had time to shout before he fired—twice. Once directly between Tom's eyes. Once left, wildly wide. Kid Mercury vanished before the first bullet even got near his forehead—and took the second in his shoulder. He collapsed onto the floor.

"Idiot. You have no training," the professor said as he stepped over Tom into my room. "You always dodge to the left. Rookie mistake. Predictable patterns only serve your enemy. Now, Paige, show me your hiding place or it's two in the head this time."

I didn't show him. I didn't. You can say I wasn't fast enough. You can say I wasn't brave enough. But I didn't give in. I pressed my hand hard against Tom's wound to stanch the bleeding. I didn't even look at Augustus.

"It's no use ignoring me," he said airily. "I can find it. There's only so many places a nasty, stupid, *bad* girl hides her filthy little diary. Under the bed? Under the mattress with her magazines? In her makeup drawer? Or have you got a loose floorboard? That *would* be a classic."

I don't read magazines. I don't have a makeup drawer. My music professor stepped daintily around the edges of my bedroom, listening for a creak, a *click*, a groan. *Please no*, I thought, and Tom locked eyes with me. *Floor of mine, just this once, shut up.*

Creak. Groan.

Dr. A leapt to the floorboard and pried it up. Tom vanished from under my hands. It happened at a speed I couldn't see, the speed of mistakes, which is faster than anything in the universe. Later, Tom told me he almost got the vials out of Augustus's hand. But he'd never been shot before. The bullet had shattered his collarbone. He didn't know how to counterbalance the damage. So, I watched as Dr. Augustus poured my hypermercury onto the ruined stump where his hand had been, rubbed it onto his bare arms and his neck like soap. He laughed, a real villain's laugh—he never had to practice once. New, silvery fingers stretched out of his scar tissue, longer and thinner and stronger than any human fingers, slicing up out of his skin like knives. He screamed. He laughed again. His eyes became diamonds.

The rest happened about how you'd expect. There's a certain inertia to these things. Heroes in motion tend to stay in motion, but villains in motion tend toward mass destruction.

Doctor Nocturne was born.

He built his machine, a great, terrible organ buried deep within the city, on which he could play out his symphony of death. With one chord, he proclaimed to every news station, he could electrify the whole of Manhattan. With another, he would bring it crashing down. Tom kept telling me to stay home. After all, I couldn't *do* anything. I couldn't help. *Just stay home and wait, Paige.* But I didn't. I couldn't. I understood how hypermercury worked, what Nocturne had done. It was my fault. I had to fix it. The last thing I said to Tom Thatcher was: *I am not going to stay home like a good little girl. I am going to beat him.*

When Tom says shit like that, the universe rearranges itself to make it true. When I said it, the universe pissed itself laughing.

They fought on the bridge. Doctor Nocturne, so much more eager to push the hypermercury past its limits than Tom had ever been, surrounded by great silver arms like a fucked-up mecha-Shiva, laughing that perfect, sick laugh, while I ran past them, small, dark, quiet, trying for once in my life to be unnoticed. One of those silver arms picked me up and flung me over the edge like I was a paper cup. The garbageman's daughter, thrown away. Oh, Tommy jumped after me. He did. My love. My hero. Caught me just in time, just before I hit the water. But a funny thing about bodies. They can't stop once they really get going. Girls in motion tend to stay in motion. Kid Mercury caught me and the sudden stop snapped my neck in half. The ends of my hair dripped out the East River onto Tom's feet and the violet lights of Doctor Nocturne's machine lit up the night and pretty soon they were the only lights left in my eyes.

Tom's got a girl now who stays home when she's told. A good girl. A girl who leaves the fixing up to him. I was just the prototype, the Act One conflict who had to go so the story could grow a little more gravitas. Some days, I'm okay with that. But some days? Some days I want to rise up out of the dark, rip open Kid Mercury's throat, and drink back every drop of my 2.21% solution, my fault, my mother, my quicksilver, my speed, my strength, my story.

But Paige Embry is dead. So, all she gets is a cigarette from one of the Hell Hath girls, plucked out of a black case. Up there, cigarettes taste like tar and ash. Down here, they taste like sunlight.

THE HELL HATH CLUB VS. THE SPACE-TIME CONTINUUM

The door to the Lethe Café swings open. A fresh gust of leafy moonlight blows in. Behind the counter, good old Neil wipes his claws on his apron and waves to the tall redhead. She vanishes before she reaches the till to place her order. When she reappears, she's a brunette. She only gets half a word out before she blinks out again. We're all used to it. Julia never stays long, but she never leaves for long, either. By the time she gets her cup of nothing, she's got a shaved head like a prisoner and she's wearing the ragged ruin of some uniform I don't recognize.

"Hi, Paige," she says shyly, scooting in next to me. "Sorry I'm late." She disappears. Reappears. Gone again. Back for more.

Julia Ash is always late.

Julia lives in the apartment across the alley from mine. She gets the *Times* and the *Deadtown Funnies* every morning. Milk delivered twice a week. Sometimes I sit on my fire escape and watch her try to make herself eggs. She flickers in and out and in and out and the yolk plops onto the floor or the counter or gets hurled against a cabinet in frustration. If the egg makes it into the pan, it always burns before she can hold on to a spatula long enough to scrape it onto a plate. Then she cries. The only way Jules ever gets breakfast is if the gargoyle who lives above her takes pity and fries her a sunny-side up on his red-hot demonic palm. His name is Christopher. He has a crocodile face and four green tongues and a high jazzy tenor. Sometimes Christopher holds her while she cries, cries and whispers: *Please let me stay. Please let me stay.*

Julia is pretty fucked up.

She lights up Deadtown style: fish a burning cig out of your purse, flick your lighter, and dark flows up to extinguish your smoke. She breathes the drifting ash.

"I can't stay," she says.

No shit. Gone. Here. Redhead. Brunette. Blonde. A bruise on her cheek. No, wait, on her shoulder. A black eye. She's always so nervous. Shaking. Clenching her hands into fists and letting go and clenching again. "Lucas gets angry if I'm not home when he gets back from work."

THE HEAT DEATH OF JULIA ASH

On Monday, I am Julia Ash. I dye my hair cranberry red and live in a trendy suburb with three cats, two teakettles, and one first edition *Jane Eyre* on which I have never once spilled ramen broth.

On Tuesday, I eat a star.

On Wednesday, I stand silently in front of a classroom at St. Ovidius's School for Wayward Children, a sensible brunette in sensible pumps, lecturing telepathically on the fall of the Byzantine Empire.

On Thursday, I tuck a platinum curl behind my ear, hit send on a new UrbanFeed article and reach over Audrey III, my ginger tabby, for my tea. She leaps away over a stack of papers, spilling a bowl of hot ramen, staining the left corner of *Jane Eyre* the color of oyster sauce.

On Friday, I am Charybdis, Insatiable Devourer of Galaxies, and my hair is the color of a nebula. I starve in space, alone, naked. I am stronger than my hunger.

On Saturday, the Millennial Men fight Lodestone in the shadows of the Antarctic ice shelf. I pulled down mountains onto his head, and we freeze to death together, his black hair and mine fusing to the lichen forever.

On Sunday, Charybdis is inside me, like a liver or a lung, but it is not me, and when it opens my mouth to swallow Arcturus, I am not responsible. It's not my *fault*. While Arcturus's planets go dark, one by one, I can smell pampas grass faintly in the burning stellar gas.

On Monday, it all begins again, the (maybe) cats and (stained or unstained) *Jane Eyre* and (possibly) St. Ovidius and my (very pressing) deadlines and the (probable) ice and the (yes or no) stars burning inside me like tea coming slowly to boil.

It's just so hard to keep everything straight when my life is being constantly edited by a madman with a bottle of cosmic Wite-Out in his fist. But every Sunday night, at 1:47 AM, he gives me fifteen minutes of Definite Reality. Some people get fifteen minutes of fame. I get fifteen minutes in the dark with the authentic, canonical universe curled up in my lap, purring away like a pulsar and wrapping its tail around my wrist.

What do you know? Look at the time.

1:47 AM

I *am* Julia Ash. I *want* to be Julia Ash. It's a relief to be her. Julia Ash is good and kind and beautiful. Julia Ash is *special*.

Julia Ash is a mockingbird.

You can call us freaks. You can call us monsters and mutants and abominations and threats to national security. But we call ourselves mockingbirds. See, when Mr. Charles Darwin sailed to Galapagos all those years ago, it wasn't the finches or the turtles that first tipped him off that some game was afoot in the genetic record. It was the mockingbirds. On those small, confined islands, mockingbirds evolved quickly enough for anyone to see with two regular old nineteenth-century human eyes. Thus, our boy Chuck began to consider the transmutation of species. And now, in the post-Darwin world, on this small, confined planet, some of us are also quick—

and strong, and full of ice and fire, and invisible, and psychic, and in flight, and invincible. We are mockingbirds. We look like you, we imitate your walk and your songs and your nests and your colors, but we are not you. We are the transmutation of species.

Professor Yes came to collect me when I was eight. When you are eight and you lock yourself in the closet, keening back and forth and sobbing for everyone to stop thinking so fucking *loud*, someone always comes to collect you. They'll wear a suit and unfashionable glasses and a Deeply Concerned Expression. Almost certainly sporting respectable, Deeply Concerned grey hair. If you're very lucky, that person will be Dr. Clara Y. Xenophile and not anybody who works for Child Protective Services or the local mental hospital.

Dr. Clara told my parents to call her Professor Yes. Everyone did, because she never said no to a child in need. She said that she understood me. She'd been troubled herself as a girl. She'd devoted her life to helping the young and the lost. She was the headmistress of a place called St. Ovidius's School for Wayward Children, which wasn't any awful Catholic laundry or Dickensian orphanage, but simply a place full of people who also understood poor little Julia. She said it all in such a nice voice that I'd already packed my bags by the time my parents thought to ask about tuition.

I sat down in Dr. Clara's long, beautiful red car. It was so quiet in there. Perfectly, absolutely quiet. No one else's thoughts banging down the doors of my head. A bottle of water and a crystal tumbler of green apple slices waited in the cupholders. Professor Yes slid in next to me. Our eyes met and held on for dear life. I liked her face. It was brown and broad and had the good kind of wrinkles that make you look like you know top-shelf stories about just *everything*. She wore her long silver hair in a big, twisty, old-fashioned bun. Suddenly, I knew she didn't need those glasses at all. She only wore them so that everyone would think she was nothing but a harmless old lady who'd done too many crosswords in her day.

Words unfurled in my brain. They didn't bang or holler or kick the can down my spinal column like everyone else's stupid thoughts. Dr. Clara's thoughts wrote themselves in lovely cursive golden letters across my cerebellum, and each letter smelled like fresh-cut green apples.

Don't tell anyone. It's our secret.

And that's how you begin to win over a child. People who share a secret share a heart.

1:49 AM

I loved school. I'd always been an obnoxious little know-it-all bookworm. But at St. Ovidius's, being a know-it-all bookworm wasn't obnoxious. I didn't have to wait until it was clear none of the other children knew the answer before I raised my hand. The moment I walked under the white stone arch with NAM VOS MUTASTIS ET ILLAS carved on it, I was home. I didn't have to pretend to be normal. I was a mockingbird, and St. Ovidius was Galapagos. I wasn't a Problem anymore.

I was a Psionic.

Just like Professor Yes.

I didn't even have to raise my hand in class anymore. Except in phys ed, which I took with the Kinetics because, after an hour of sweating and crying in Professor Yes's office, I lifted the little bronze phoenix statue on her desk a couple of inches into the air without touching it. It floated there for six whole seconds before it burst into glops of ultraviolet lava. The Professor was so impressed, she frowned. That constant, reassuring, kindergarten-teacher smile just bolted off her face and she looked like someone else completely. But I was just as shocked. I didn't even know I could do that until I did. Maybe that should be carved on the white stone arch instead. It probably sounds impressive in Latin.

But as the years went on, the Psionic/Kinetic curriculum stopped challenging me. It sounds awful, but I was bored. I course-hopped all over the school. Elementals, Shifters, Mechanicals, even the constantly changing halls of the Ontologics Wing, where the kids who could spank time and turn reality into a paper airplane practiced on the unsuspecting masonry.

I remember sitting in the common room with Henry Hart, a boy so beautiful, he'd done national commercials before he accidentally ignited the overbearing director of a Frosty Frogs spot and Professor Yes came to collect him. Everybody knew his face, even if they couldn't always quite remember where they'd seen him before. I met Henry because we both hated running. Sure, gym class meant shooting fireballs into a basketball hoop and turning the bleachers to ice, then a waterfall, then a jungle, then back again, but it also meant plain old boxing and volleyballs-to-the-face and running laps. Henry and I both dragged our feet on the big gravelly track, halfheartedly jogging if a teacher saw us slacking. I knew who he was right away, but I never said anything. There's no such thing as before St. Ovidius. We were in love before we finished the thousand meters.

We were twelve. In the common room, at night, we were twelve. In big green armchairs with brass bolts in the arms, drinking (decaf) coffee like Real Live Grown-Ups, we were twelve. Henry balanced a cozy little fireball on the back of his fingers, making it hop from knuckle to knuckle.

"That's awesome," I said, dazzled by the nearness of him. "Your control's gotten so much better."

Henry scowled. Sometimes when a person scowls, it ruins their face, makes them look cruel, but not Henry. "It's nothing," he snapped.

"What do you mean, nothing? You're a glorious deity of fire and you know it."

He looked up out of his green armchair, his mouth all screwed up like he was going to cry. "It's *nothing*. *I'm* nothing. I can't do anything a cheap flamethrower can't do. Maybe a hundred years ago I'd be a . . . a superhero. A legend. But now? You can buy me at an army surplus store for $49.99 plus tax. And you don't have to feed a flamethrower fifty bacon cheeseburgers a day to keep it firing." Henry needed calories. He needed saturated fat. It autolyzed his combustive enzymes or something. "I'm not like *you*."

I stared at my knees to keep him from seeing the shame rolling down my cheeks.

He rushed over to me, knocking over his coffee onto an ethics textbook (onto a first edition copy of *Jane Eyre*). "No, no, Jules, that's not what I meant. I mean . . . you're really something else. You can't buy a Julia Ash off the shelf anywhere, at any price. I'm a mockingbird. You're the HMS *Beagle*."

I still wasn't like everyone else, not really. I wouldn't find the end of what I could do until years later, at the edge of a white dwarf star.

1:51 AM

I met everyone I ever loved at St. Ovidius.

We got to pick new names when we graduated. My friends stopped being Henry Hart and Lachlan Reed and Lana Kowalski and became a pantheon: the Silver Siren, Zigzag, Pell-Mell, the Maroon Marauder, Snow Queen, Whitewater, Paravox, Ha'Penny. Hal Cyon. Bruce Force. Crucible.

Henry. My Crucible.

After graduation, Professor Yes called a group of us into her office. The melted chunks of the bronze phoenix I'd exploded still sat on her desk. We sat down—me, Crucible, Bruce Force, Hal Cyon, Zigzag, and Paravox. I was the only girl. I tried not to let it bother me. It was time to take the next step, Professor Yes told us. To use our powers for good instead of spinning our wheels. She was putting together a team. The best of us. To fight, not crime or mustached evildoers or endemic social inequality, but other mockingbirds. Mockingbirds who wanted to expose us or enslave everyday normals like our parents. Or just plain rule the world, like some people had always done, long before any of them could fly. In time, there'd be dozens of us, but just then, in that office, while I stared at the clumps of phoenix on her mahogany desk with the smell of green apples swimming in my brain, we were only six. The Millennial Men. We were going to make a better world.

For a while, that's just what we did. Hal Cyon trapped Doctor Nocturne in a pocket dimension stuffed inside the blue whale in the Museum of Natural History. Crucible burned down the lair of the Rat Bastard with his army of mutated rodents inside. Zigzag got to Victor Volatile's Boomsday Device just in time and cut the wires with his razor breath. The Clock of Ages changed the timeline so that none of us ever met—and Paravox changed it back with one arm tied behind his back. Bruce Force just beat the hell out of anyone and chomped his cigar while he did it. I personally erased the eight-sided mind of the Arachnochancellor and disintegrated his webship. We battered Miasma in the streets of Guignol City while his mustard-gas golems hissed and spat under every stoplight. But mostly we fought Lodestone, Professor Yes's nemesis, a mastermind right out of our textbooks, able to command stone from the depths of the earth and bent on bringing all mockingbirds under his control. Their war began long before any of us were born.

Of course, they always came back somehow. Doctor Nocturne rode that blue whale into a crowd of philanthropists and turned them all into philanthrozombies. Victor Volatile built a new laboratory on the moon. Lodestone always slipped through our fingers, his iron face disappearing back into the shadows. But that was the game. We grew strong. *I* grew strong. It made everyone nervous, but I couldn't see why. Isn't stronger better? Would they all have whispered like that if Bruce suddenly sprouted new powers? I doubted it. The world likes a big man punching things to get bigger and punch harder. But even Crucible got quiet when I came into a room by the time the whole disaster with Sergeant Pluto started darkening the edges of our little family portrait.

Some Sundays, I wonder why the Millennials agreed so easily to be Professor Yes's personal matadors. They don't call her that because she never says no to a child in need. They call her that because she can make anyone do whatever she likes. Say no to drugs; say yes to Professor Yes. Her psionic strength beats even mine. Of course she'd never *do* it.

That would be wrong.

She wouldn't.

1:53 AM

By the Terrible No Good Very Cosmically Significant Day, I could fly.

Flying is weird. The first time I did it, I got airsick. Flying doesn't *feel* like flying. It feels like the sky is inside you and hates the earth so much, it wants to rescue you. The worst thing is the cold. It's brutal up there. My hair freezes, my eyebrows, my eyelashes—I have to thaw them slowly in the sauna or it shatters into a million dark red pieces. Flying in space is worse.

When I say the words *flying in space,* you don't really think about it much. An action in a place. Right. Fine. Julia flew through space. But once you've snorted a line of physics and punched a hole in escape velocity, you're not *flying* at all anymore. There's no wind to ride, no storms to stow away on. Up there, you're not a bird; you're a ship. Your skin goes hard, crystalline, you stop needing to breathe, and your endocrine system shifts into propulsion mode. And you roar through the stars. There's no up or down or end to anything. Eddies of radiation and stray gravity and microscopic debris spin around you like ribbons on a maypole. It hurts the whole time.

Only Zigzag and I can do it, out of the lot of us. But Zigzag was born that way—a nuclear-powered engine in a pixieish boy's body. I just kept going one day and by the time I looked behind me, I had made it past the Kuiper Belt. The point is, none of it would ever have happened to Zig, who'd been best friends with space since he was playing with plastic soldiers three feet above his mother's backyard.

We were coming back from victory on Mars. Lodestone had built a new city under a diamond dome on the red sand of Isidis Planitia, a city where mockingbirds could live in peace—so long as they lived by his law. We pulled down his statue onto the long red central boulevard of Lodria Prime, and I swear I only thought for a moment of how nice it might be to live in this place, where we wouldn't have to hide. Lodestone himself escaped into a maze of underground tunnels, but all in all, we'd had a very satisfactory Monday. Zigzag and I raced each other through the black while the others napped on their fancy Falk Industries rocket, fitted out with mints on every pillow. The sun winked and sparkled on the hem of Zig's violet cape, on the glass edge of the Earth, on the crags of the moon. I wasn't paying attention. I was happy. I ran right into it, like a deer and an eighteen-wheeler.

Later, Professor Yes said it must have been a solar flare, but that's bullshit. I caught something up there, but it didn't come from the sun. I felt it slide over me and around me and into me, the color of hunger, the color of the future and the past, the color of the Galapagos Sea.

Its name was Charybdis.

I shivered electric. I tried to call out to Zigzag, to the Millennial rocket disappearing far ahead of me, but all that came out of my mouth was fire and geometry. I vaporized into infinite particles, each cell of me, briefly, fully sentient and screaming.

I rematerialized in my parents' living room. They were at work. Only the dog saw me. Hard winter sunlight streamed through windows I hadn't seen in years. I turned on the radio; David Bowie told me to shut my mouth. I opened the cabinet—they still had the clay mug I'd made in second grade. It was shaped like an elephant, but the trunk broke off in the kiln. I made myself a cup of coffee, but when I tried to drink it, my two-creams-one-sugar turned into red Martian dust. I poured Mars out into the sink. A thin white stalk spooled up out of the sand and opened into a flower on fire.

"Huh," I said.

Everything had changed.

1:55 AM

At first, it was all *fantastic*, just *splendid*, what a gift for the cause! Professor Yes was perfectly happy to wheel me out on the showroom floor, a mockingbird who'd flown past all her limits and become an eagle, a hawk, a 747. The metaphors fell down. I was the biggest gun she had, and, for a while, she aimed me everywhere. There were no rules. I reached out one hand toward Sergeant Pluto and he disintegrated into a hundred shades of the color green. I wept and cities rebuilt themselves. I laughed and Victor Volatile turned into a new inland sea somewhere in North Dakota. Nobody had a problem with the new Julia as long as she did their chores for them. Kept the world nice and tidy, took the rubbish out, dusted off the minimalist black-and-white discussion piece morality had become.

They turned on me, eventually. Oh, they were so *concerned*, my boys. Only for my own good, only because they were so *worried* about my delicate constitution!

"She can't control it," Paravox whispered to the Professor.

"No one could," Bruce hurried to say, so I wouldn't take it personally.

"The more she uses her powers, the less *human* she gets," Hal Cyon sighed, looking so fucking earnest while he called me less than human. So fucking sincere.

"What the fuck, Hal," I snapped. "You can turn into a time-traveling dragon. How human are you?"

Crucible couldn't even look at me. "Maybe if you could just . . . hold back a little. Until you can figure out exactly what happened out there and whether it's hurting her."

They all stood around Professor Yes's desk like veterinarians discussing a rowdy horse in need of breaking.

"Since when," I said softly, "is power a problem for any of you?"

"You don't understand," Zigzag pleaded.

I stared them all down. "Sure I do. Hold back. Got it."

If you could just wait until it's clear that none of the other children know the answer before raising your hand. Don't read ahead of the rest of the class. No one likes a know-it-all.

Finally, Lodestone met the Millennials on the shores of Antarctica. Neutral ground. I floated above the snow. Whales came blinking out of the deeps to croon at me. I sang Bowie to them in the concert halls of their vast salted minds. We waited for Lodestone's army, his twisted, angry mockingbirds, our opposite numbers. But the army didn't come. Lodestone himself strode over the Ross Ice Shelf in his long silver cloak and his iron mask. He had one companion. A tall young man wearing white punk gear tourniqueted with straps of leather and rope, his head half shaved and half curling, shining black hair. His eyes were stitched savagely shut; two angry black X's scrawled over them from brow to cheekbone. Those horrible, furious black X's glowered all over his body, hundreds of them, big and small, shakily scribbled and boldly slashed and some carved into his flesh with knives. He didn't seem to feel the cold; he carried no weapons.

His name was Retcon. He was new. He was strong. He was about to ruin my life.

I held back at first. I wanted Crucible and Bruce Force and the others to feel *useful*. I seethed, but I'm a team player. I always was. A nice girl doesn't show off. Crucible lit up Lodestone in a column of fire; Zigzag darted around, too fast to see; Hal's scales flipped up over his skin like playing cards. Paravox started incanting, his eyes turning to molten glass. Bruce went after Retcon with his blades.

But the new guy didn't flinch. He dodged Bruce easily, casually, like he'd meant to bend practically in half anyway, and if it just happened to keep him out of the path of death, so much the better. He turned his awful stitched-up eyes to me. His mind hit mine. I knew he could see me. I knew his name. I knew with a sickening feeling in my gut that somehow he had fought this battle, this exact frigid, miserable fight, many times before. It was only new for us. Retcon spoke into the star-storm of my mind:

Hiya, Jules! Watch this!

Retcon reached up and dragged one long, sharp fingernail over his brown shoulder once, twice. A black X rose up on his skin as though he'd had a schoolkid's Magic Marker up one sleeve.

Crucible burst into flames.

The fire that had never hurt Henry Hart, had always loved him and done whatever he asked, swallowed him whole. His skin blistered, scorched, peeled away. His bones cracked like kindling. I saw it all, I heard it all, I felt him die the way I always felt everything that had ever happened to him. I screamed—I *became* a scream. Nothing in me was not that scream. And the scream of me clawed reality apart. It threw Retcon north toward Buenos Aires at the speed of sound. It annihilated Lodestone's mind and replaced it with the mind of a twelve-year-old Egyptian girl from the height of the Middle Kingdom. The scream of me dragged green grass and wildflowers out of the million-year freeze of the ice shelf and I fell onto that meadow, sobbing red Mars dust onto the warm, wet earth.

1:58 AM

So, yes. I lost it after Antarctica. I didn't quit. I just . . . didn't show up for work. I checked into a hotel in Buenos Aires and put a DO NOT DISTURB sign over my life. Professor Yes grazed my mind with phantom fingers, her green apple–scented thoughts searching for mine across the sea. I would not let her in. The TV clicked on in my room, the screen filled up with her miserable, stupid face, that fake maternal smile.

"Come home, Julia," she said, her voice dripping with shit

and kindness. I rolled over in the sweatheap of my griefbed and vaporized the television. I opened up the liquor cabinet of my head enough to lob one whiskey-bottle thought at her:

This is what happens when I hold back, Clara.

But I wouldn't hold back again. I wouldn't keep my hand down for one more second. I did whatever I wanted. I let the thing inside me, the thing that had grabbed hold of me somewhere between home and Mars, run wild. I turned the Casa Rosada into a ziggurat, then a pumpkin, then a very confused alpaca. I listened in on everyone in a way I hadn't done since before St. Ovidius, sucking up their sticky, wadded-up little secrets. I drank and fucked anyone I could find and passed out in the street, a goddess sleeping in her own puke with a bag of old bread for a pillow, fighting the birds for it, setting the bolder ones on fire if they got too close. But then the fire would remind me, and the cobblestones shook and the sky went black and Henry died all over again in my head until I beat my skull against a friendly wall long enough to lose consciousness again.

Professor Yes followed me everywhere. She appeared on billboards, on the radio, in the pages of books, every word and image warping into hers.

Come home, Julia. Don't do this to yourself.

We can't just let someone like you run free, sweetheart. You're not safe.

I think the fucking bothered the team the most. Every time I dragged someone home to make me feel real, the hotel room mirrors and microwave and appalling pastel paintings would explode with a hundred disapproving Professors. I ignored her. Who cared? Why should we all be with the same idiots we loved in high school? Dead idiots. Idiots on fire. A church window with Clara's big dumb eyes tut-tutted that perhaps I was drawing some kind of terrible power from all these men, taking their souls, their anima. As if that was the only reason to let so many of them climb on top of me.

Leave me alone, you Puritan fucking outhouse. I shattered the window with a stomp of my shoes on the morning frost. They all thought that. I could hear them thinking that. I could hear Bruce Force thinking that at a goddamn strip club, but I couldn't hear anyone thinking he was sucking those dancers dry. And neither was I. It was just sex. And loneliness. And hunger. And the utter nihilism of another human body.

I found Retcon in the basement of a shitty little casino. He'd crashed into it when I threw him; they didn't have the cash to fix it up quite yet. He turned his head toward me. His thoughts didn't smell like green apples. They smelled like wild grass and hot stone.

Heya, Jules. I missed you. Don't hit me too hard.

I hit him. Again and again. Against the dark slot machines, the roulette wheels, the card tables. Harder than any human and most mockingbirds could take. He let me. It all bounced off him. Retcon looked up at me from under the billiards with his ruined eyes and scrawled out another nasty X on the back of his hand.

The casino vanished.

Retcon and I stood in a field of pampas grass and big purple flowers. Massive prehistoric capybaras grazed on the plains. A few mooed in dim Mesozoic alarm. The sun was setting in red splatters.

"Where are we?" I was too stunned to swear at him, or even to finish the punch I'd been winding up.

Retcon turned to me with wide-open, bright blue, unstitched eyes. "We're about a thousand years back in a timeline where the New World was never colonized. Europe just sort of . . . didn't happen. Africa's aces, though. We should go have a look."

"Why did you bring me here?" I clenched my fist again.

"Hold on, hold on!" Retcon held up his hands. No tricks. "I brought you here because I've always brought you here. I will always have been bringing you here. I've met a hundred million versions of you. I know you *so* well. This is what I do. This is what I *did*. Back on the ice. I moved us all into a timeline where Crucible wasn't invulnerable to fire. There's another one where he never had any powers at all, where no one ever did. You're still together in that one. You have a baby girl. She's going to be a programmer when she grows up. In this timeline, our Henry is . . ." Retcon scanned the herds. He pointed. "Just there. Alive and well."

The Crucible-capybara mooed gently at the rising moon and scratched at his haunches.

"Fine. I'm impressed. So move me back to my timeline. The good timeline."

"It's one-way, I'm afraid. But doesn't it feel better knowing that somewhere, your Henry, the one who called you a boat, is alive and safe?"

No, it did not. But I didn't say anything. I walked toward the capybaras, soothing them with the tendrils of my mind, singing Bowie into their cozy, hungry hearts. I held out my hand to the Henry-beast. He looked suspicious. He'd never smelled human this close before unless the human smell was very quickly followed by the blood smell. But then he nuzzled my palm and gave it a prim little lick. Somewhere deep, in every timeline, Henry Hart knows me.

Retcon ran his hand over the shaved half of his head. "I didn't know him. He wasn't anything to me. Just a job. You've had lots of jobs. Your jobs have killed my friends, too, you know. My family. But I knew you didn't mean anything by it. It's not personal.

When you see all of time and space, you can be very understanding. I hope you will understand too. In that timeline, the one I took us out of, Crucible would have siphoned off some of your power to keep you from—he thought—going mad, and eventually, he would have lit the world on fire with it. Destroyed us all. I was helping. I *am* helping."

"I don't believe you." Crucible nibbled at my sleeve. "Just take me home."

"Okay." Retcon shrugged. "But in your timeline, they're going to kill you. Well, not kill you. But freeze you and bury you in a bunker. You're too powerful for her to let you live. Professor Yes doesn't tolerate mockingbirds she can't control. Come on, you must know that. You are the knife she uses to cull the flock. She's done with you. You have to go in the drawer."

"*Fuck*," I sighed. Tears came up in my eyes. The dark spilled out over the long, pale grass. Stars like infinite timelines broke the sky apart into light. "Whose side are you on?"

"Reality's."

I chewed on that for a few minutes. "What happened to your stitches?"

Retcon put a tentative hand on my hair. It didn't feel so bad. Human contact is a terrible drug. Sometimes, you'll even take the hit you know is tainted. You can't stop yourself. The need is too strong. "There's too many people in most timelines. I see all their versions crowding in on top of each other, all trying to happen at once, all fighting to *become*. But here, there's just us. Here, I can open my eyes."

We stayed there for months. Years. Mockingbirds don't age much. It's hard to tell. We built a yurt. Capybara-Crucible stayed near me always, looking up at me with big brown capybara eyes, his thoughts as peaceful and wordless as sleep. We ate wildcat and otter and tapir. We drank cold river water. Retcon told me his real name: Lucas Fawn. We flew across the ocean to see the metropolises of Africa once, but neither of us could bear so many other minds so close by. Eventually, we made love under a majaguillo tree. That sounds bad, I know. But Lucas let me roam the whole of his mind. I could see what he saw, time crackling like ice on the surface of an infinite lake. I could understand. I touched him and the X's on his skin turned into the word *REST*, written neatly, over and over.

When we finished, I stretched sleepily in the warm summer wind. Lucas and I took the long way round the river to our yurt, holding hands, companionably quiet. Something loosened in me, something that had been clenched tight as a fist since Henry died. I smiled at Retcon and kissed his cheek. It would be good to sleep, for once. I knew I'd have no dreams at all. I lifted the flap of the yurt.

And walked into the white icefield of the Antarctic. The Millennials ranged all around me, screaming, yelling commands, warnings. Bruce slashed at a figure in an iron mask. Paravox was chanting, his eyes filling up with molten glass. And Crucible, my Crucible, my Henry, my heart, alive and whole, threw fire from his hands at a tall young man with X's drawn over his eyes. Lucas smiled sadly at me, a smile I'd come to know so well and so long.

I thought it was a gift. *Make things right. Take it all back.*

What could I do? I was such a big fucking problem for all of them. My power, my strength, my lonely body. They'd freeze me and bury me in a bunker. Or Crucible would siphon off some of my power—my *soul*, as if any of them had the right—and light the world on fire. Any girl who wanted in on Team Millennial after me would have to prove she was weak enough to put the boys at ease. I had no good choices on Earth. So, I picked up Henry in my arms and shot into the sky. I was gone before Lodestone could cry out. I set Henry Hart down in Buenos Aires, by an elegant little casino. I kissed him. He looked at me in confusion, big brown eyes full of love and questions.

I disappeared. Up. Into the black and the white and the cold and the fire. Into space, into crystal flesh and breathless speed. As long and far as I could go. I gave in to the mass of magic and molten physics inside me. The alien, churning thing I'd crushed down inside myself like sorrow. I became the piece of broken irradiated sun that caught me coming home from Mars, the seed of another creature I swallowed in space: Charybdis, a whirlpool of want and need and sacrifice. I remembered a billion years of travel in the shrieking dark. I remembered feasts of worlds before the invention of self-replicating cellular life. I remembered a singularity of hate and fury and hunger.

I forgot who Julia was.

I flew a long way.

2:00 AM

Two minutes left. I am Julia Ash. I am Julia Ash.

I am Charybdis.

I am so hungry.

This was Lodestone's plan. He used me no more or less than Professor Yes. I have been nothing but a gun all my life.

I ate a star. It seemed like a good idea at the time. I was starving. The whirlpool inside me could not keep going with only a roast beef lunch and/or the phantom tapir jerky of another lifetime to fuel it. When you're hungry, really ravenous, you eat everything in sight. You barely even taste it. Your whole body is a mouth. I couldn't help it. I couldn't see anything but the famine of my personal universe. I couldn't see anything but that blue star, hanging in the dark like meat. I opened my jaw as wide as light-years and bit into it. The star-juice ran down my chin. I couldn't hear the screaming of planets suddenly freezing in the void, careening in the release of gravity's hand brake. I couldn't hear it, I swear. Charybdis was so much bigger than a planet's weeping.

And then it was gone. The Galapagos-colored thing that had filled me up for so long. It was satisfied. The red dust and the coffee and David Bowie and green in the Antarctic and the flower on fire in the sink. All gone. All the lights gone out in Georgia. I began to fall out of the sky.

I fell a long way.

On Sunday nights, at 1:47 AM, for fifteen minutes, I know what happened. They had to punish me. Of course they did. But they never understood. There may have been a universe in which Crucible was vulnerable to fire, but Retcon couldn't really move everyone there wholesale. He and Lodestone planned it so beautifully. Retcon dropped me into a bubble of experience, a bubble of grief in Buenos Aires, broken slot machines, Clara Y. Xenophile's face staring at me out of a rabbit-eared television, untouched pampas and wild capybaras and the majaguillo tree. Retcon knew I would do anything to save Henry, to avoid living it all again, to spare everyone, to save everyone.

All I ever wanted to do is save everyone.

And that's how Lodestone aimed me, cocked me, and fired me at a star on the other side of the galaxy. God knows who he hated enough on those planets to turn off their sun, but he got what he wanted. And after it was all done, Retcon, a new player, ready to consider his allegiances objectively, could come humbly, hat in hand, to St. Ovidius and that big mahogany desk and the lumps of exploded bronze phoenix and offer to take care of the Julia problem as only he could.

After all, he was on reality's side.

On Sunday nights, at 1:47 AM, I know I have lived in Retcon's prison for seven years. Flickering through recycled realities, losing myself in myself, over and over. I know that they've all forgotten me. Redemption is for other people. For literally everyone else. Mockingbirds fuck things up. Occupational hazard. No one locked up Avast when he inundated Los Angeles to get at one lousy shark. But I am the Wayward Child of St. Ovidius. I was used and tricked and thrown away, but I cannot be forgiven.

It's a funny thing. You go your whole life thinking you're the protagonist, but really, you're just backstory. The boys shrug and go on, they fight and blow things up and half of them do much worse than a star and still get the key to the city, and eventually you're just a story your high school boyfriend tells the kid he had with his new wife.

Every day, Retcon crosses out my past and rewrites it, drawing a furious black X over me again and again. Some days, he even lets me be innocent, lets Charybdis take the blame out into the black and set it on fire. He can probably do it without thinking, like a digestive process. Lucas Fawn goes about his day, redeemed, eating and drinking with my friends, in my house, and some autonomic system erases me for the thirteen thousandth time, while another builds a new Julia or a new Charybdis to play with in his private dollhouse. Some guilty, some innocent, some powerless, some young, some broken, some dead.

Maybe someday he'll find a version that can get free.

• • •

2:02 AM

I am Julia Ash. I dye my hair cranberry red and live in a trendy suburb with three cats, two teakettles, and one first edition *Jane Eyre* on which I have never once spilled ramen broth.

Lucas is coming home from work early today. It's his birthday. He called from the train.

Can't wait to see you, Jules!

I start slicing onions for pasta carbonara, his favorite. I glance nervously at the clock. I don't know if it'll be ready in time. I start to tremble. Lucas hates it when I'm late with dinner.

The cake rises slowly in the oven, filling the apartment with the smell of home.

THE HELL HATH CLUB VS. THE EVIL CLOWN

The dead do eat.

Some habits are just too hard to break. Besides, the infinite wasteland of linear time would well and truly suck without the occasional Taco Tuesday. Gotta pass the time somehow. The trick of it is, the only aisle in the Deadtown Grocery is Extinct Meat and Veg—we can't have it down here till you're done with it up there. The milk Julia gets delivered every week? That's fresh, creamy quagga milk, with a side of great auk eggs over easy. I know a gargoyle named Dave who's got a big black cart down by Elysium Park and sells triceratops pies and white rhino po' boys with a side of hot fries made from a Peruvian blue potato that peaced out before Columbus was a twinkle in Queen Isabella's eye. Dave fucking loves pop music, and he'll swap you a saber-toothed burrito for whatever sweet, sweet lyrics you've still got banging around your skull. And Dave don't discriminate—Duran Duran, Les Miz, Streisand, Weird Al, he wants it all. So, good news! All those earworms and cheesy choruses that soaked up valuable brain space and kept you from remembering even one single phone number will, eventually, be worth their weight in beer-battered coelacanth.

But we don't *have* to. You can't exactly starve in Deadtown. We don't even really have appetites, and even Dave's prehistoric fish and chips don't make us feel full. Everything tastes a little thin, a little slight. It's more like we were buried with the *memory* of the *idea* of hunger, and now it's stuck to us like old toilet paper.

So, it's weird how much Pauline Ketch eats.

She orders everything and just goes to town, powering through medium-rare thylacine steaks and blue amaranth waffles and deep-fried dodo, Taliaferro apple pie with mammoth-milk ice cream, velociraptor corn dogs and corned-aurochs-and-hash and thunder-bird piccata with Babylonian lemon sauce. Neil can barely keep up. Sometimes, I think she must have been a binge-and-purger when she was alive; she's skinny as a matchstick. Now that she's dead, it's all binge. The big purge has already come and gone. Pauline grins at us over her plates; juice drips down over the scars on her chin. She winks one of her crazy eyes at me. She got them tattooed and painted to look like a commedia dell'arte puppet three weeks into a zombie plague. Pauline tears into a pan-seared fillet of Steller's sea cow and moans with pleasure, as though it tastes just the same as supper back home, as though she isn't a ghost gobbling up ghosts. She makes a pouty face at Julia and bats her eyelashes.

"Cheer up, chickies! Just 'cause you're dead don't mean you gotta be so damn *dull*! Waa waa, my boyfriend didn't save me! My husband was a meanie! Who cares? I ask ya! Lookit all these blub-berin' MUGS! Why the long fuckin' faces, Mrs. Horsey and Miss Nag? Halfa you got mouths like sour candy and the other half're gonna bust somethin' if you don't catch a train to Coolville on the lickety-split. You wanna Valium? Percocet? Xanax? Ativan? Oxy? I think I got some in my purse."

A blond girl named Daisy and my friend in the green gloves shrug and hold out their hands. Pauline giggles.

"Naw, I'm only foolin'. I got nothin'. Pockets like a hobo clown.

They don't let ya bring the fun stuff down here to D Ward! Deadtown Pharmacy only has one prescription and it's for Mr. Place E. Bo, and that guy is a *dick*. What I wouldn't give for a nice bouquet of benzos with whipped cream on top, am I right, ladies? Ladies?" Pauline throws down her fork. "This is the worst group therapy *ever*. You're all against me, and WHY? 'Cause I'm a bad girl. Ooooo, so scary! You're all so pretty and perfect and tragic, aren't you? Not me. I'm a cherry bomb with a go-fuck-yourself fuse and a soul like a stubbed-out cigarette. Well, what's being good ever got ya? Huh? That's what I thought. Sorry, we're full up on Madonnas around here. Time for the whore to come out and slay." Pauline slings her arm around Julia's pale shoulders. "Aw, come on! Didn'tya ever wanna *try* it? Just the once? Oh, baby, everyone's doin' it. It feels so *good*. If you loved me, you would. I promise I'll still respect you in the morning. Don't you listen to those prudes. It doesn't hurt. Just slip on something black and low-cut, carve yourself the biggest goddamn slice of whatever cake they said you couldn't have, and be a VILLAIN for a night! Come on. You know they deserve it. You know they ALL deserve it. What's the use of all that rage you got if you don't take it out for a spin? You just sit here by me. Pretty Polly knows how to drive stick."

Daisy laughs, a short, sharp bark, but not because anything's funny. She laughs because she finally remembers where she's seen Pauline Ketch before. Pauline drinks that hollow laugh like root beer.

"Yeah, that's me. You want my autograph, hot stuff? I'm famous! Pretty Polly, born Pauline Ketch, High Hellion of Guignol City, bank blower-upper and cop knocker-downer, professional punk, voted Most Likely to Piss in Grimdark's Sad Black Cornflakes, and the hottest little bat in Mr. Punch's belfry. I'm not like the rest of you. Deadtown's a pit stop. I'm in, I'm out, PRESTO-CHANGO! Poof! Now you see me, now I'm back in Alivetown, putting on my stockings. *My* man's coming back for me. He's nothing like your sad-sack pizza delivery boys, over it and dancin' on yer grave in thirty minutes or less! My baby's not gonna forget about *me*, no siree! Any minute, you'll see. Mr. Punch is gonna grab onta me and never let go."

THE TRAGICAL COMEDY OR COMICAL TRAGEDY OF PAULINE KETCH

I met my baby the old-fashioned way—in prison! Good ol' Sarkomand Sanatorium, my home away from home. Aw, I still miss Christmases in B Ward! Candy canes, sleigh bells, and Santa Claus the electroshock therapist! He brings suction cups and pretty blue wires for ALL the good boys and girls! B Ward is the Extra Very Doubly Special Barbie Dreamhouse for Violent Offenders, and golly, the whole gang was there! Rat Bastard, Miasma, Doctor Nocturne, Six Figure, the Fearwig, Megalodon . . . all the greats!

Now, you might think I'm nothin' but a coupla guns and a silver medal in gymnastics, but I got me a superpower, too.

I can make anybody like me for about five minutes.

Ten if I try hard. It always goes to shit after that. Can't help it, the real me just squirts out all over the place, and the real me is real hard to get off your shoes. But you can get *crazy* far in this world on the back of somebody thinkin' you're just the best girl ever for five minutes a pop.

Never worked on my dad, though. I guess that's what you call a weakness. Like what's-his-name and those stupid green crystals. Daddums took one look at me in the nursery and knew everything he needed to know: I wasn't a boy and I was bad. Buh-buh-buh-bad to the bone. He told the doc: *Better not turn the lights off in there at night. Anything could happen.* Thanks a bunch, Daddy Ketch! Oh sure, he was *right*, but maybe he wouldn't'ta been if I hadn't heard that shit with my cute little baby ears, you know?

So, naturally, I burned our fancy house down when I was twenty-one. Anything can happen if you believe in yourself! Then I ran away and burned some *other* fancy-people stuff down, and just when I was settlin' into the arsonist's lifestyle real nice, some dumb ox in body armor knocked me on the head while I was enjoying a nice post-exploded-country-club cigarette. But rich girls don't go to jail! Rich girls aren't *criminals*, don't you know? They're just *troubled*, poor things. So, Daddy's fat shiny name got me shipped over to Dr. Leng's personal freak show.

Pops walked me up the garden path to Sarkomand. Used to be some other richie's pad, tacky fake-Greek statues all over the place, full of filthy old windows, roof all scrunched up like there was a going-outta-gables sale. I skipped along and laced my fingers in his and swung our hands and said:

"Aw, Daddy, d'ya think the other kids will like me? D'ya think I'll make a friend on the very first day? D'ya think I'll be the teacher's pet?"

And he didn't say shit because he never even liked me for five minutes in my whole life. He is a *Bad Daddy*.

B Ward's got a common area we called the Pool. Used to be a natatorium. That's how ya say giant fuck-off swimming pool in richie-speak. Still covered in tile from floor to ceiling, only now green and blue mold has crapped up the caulk, layin' down a fuzzy, scuzzy grid of filth like the rot wants ta play tic-tac-toe with the ghost of dead ol' Mrs. Sarkomand, who went totally bug-faced whacko and told everyone she was a mermaid and had to stay WET, don't you understand, WET, WET, WET! So Mistah Sarko

built the natatorium to keep his wife wet. Hot. I swear, rich folks' lives are so dumbfuck deluxified, they read like dirty fairy tales. And I oughta know! I ain't nothin' but a porno starring Hansel and Gretel and a big bad hungry creature in a candy cane house.

The Pool is a giant, damp, echoey dump. Long grimy windows let about a loogey's worth of light in. All the *good* boys and girls lay around on long chairs like a boy's gonna bring 'em a daiquiri any minute. The *bad* boys and girls get their shit wheeled on down to the bottom of Mrs. Sarkomand's therapy pool and parked till some fat fart factory remembers to come back and get them. They spend all day just starin' at the tiles and rusted ladders dropping down three steps into the air. The water's long gone, but Dr. Leng does love what's left—nine and a half feet of slick moldy unclimbable blue tile. Get down and stay down, puppers! I usedta see Miasma walkin' up and down the lanes like he was swimming laps. That dude's a *freak*, I'll tell you what.

But I hadn't done anything naughty that first day, so I got to stay up top in Club Meds. All us well-behaved bitches drugged to the gills and layin' out like crazy could give us a tan. When ya think about it, people on the outside pay good money to get that wasted and have that little to do. I figured I could swing Sarkomand, no problem. Wasn't much going in the Pool when I made my grand debut. A coupla dead ferns in one corner, an old Candy Land game nobody played, and a soggy paperback library fulla murderbooks and fuckfic potboilers donated by some League of Old Ladies. Old ladies and young punks don't love a damn thing but sex and death. All the rest of this garbage-can world is for the dorks in between.

Gosh, I wasn't anybody then! I didn't even have a *nom de crime* picked out or *nothin'*! Just an eager-to-please firebug with a nice haircut and manufacturer-warranteed daddy issues. I checked out my new digs—what a buncha heartthrobs! Of course, they were pretty much *compost mentis.* The Arachnochancellor had some drool plopping out of one side of his mouth. Dinochrome was all glazed over and rusted straight to hell. I knew 'em all by name.

Except the fella in the corner by the ferns. Mistah Man over there was one long, tall, funny-lookin' drinka water! Hair like radioactive lemonade and red eyes—*really* red! Like two big beautiful stoplights burnin' up his skull. But no light in the world ever stopped me. He stared straight ahead, slumped over like a puppet after the big show, with that dreamy Thorazine gaze I'd come to love. What can I say? Damaged calls to damaged.

I sauntered on over to the night warden, Nurse Happy. Honest to lollipops, that actually was her name! Said it right on her badge: *Wilhemina Happi*. Finnish or somethin'. Anyways, I put on my superpower like a paira specs. It's easy. Like when you wanna pet a fella's dog but the dog's growlin' and puttin' his ears back so you hold your hand out for it to sniff and talk real sweet. 'Cause everybody's somebody's dog, you know. It's even easier for girls. Daddy never got that. Never clocked how being a girl is a sneaky kinda mutant power. Pops was stuck in the old world, where the only superpower worth having was being a white straight boy. And fuck me if I still wouldn't take that over some doofy bow-and-arrow tricks. But I work with what I got. See, people got this bright, shiny picture of what a Friendly Girl looks like in their head. Funny thing is, everybody's got the same picture! All you gotta do is shimmy till you look like the picture and presto-chango, you're a Friendly Girl! Folks just give you their love in a basket. And when you're done takin' it all, you can just go invisible and fade away—all girls come with that power preinstalled. Watch me do my thing, kittens! I made my eyes all big and wide and glisteny, slouched so

I didn't look so tall, dipped my head down so's nobody could feel threatened by little ol' me, showed my open hands—no tricks, Ma! Sniff it up! I finished myself off with a shy little schoolgirl smile, the kind that makes teacher wanna give ya some *special attention* so you can reach your full potential. Then I blushed—I can do that anytime I want. Like puttin' on paint. *What's a girl like me doin' in a place like this?*

Nurse Happy ate it all up with a shovel. I scrubbed my voice clean and pink before I said anything.

"I . . . I think it's time for my medication, Nurse Happy."

There's no numbers on the clocks in Sarkomand. They say it's easy for people like me to get obsessed with numbers, with time. But it's pretty much always time for your medication in the Pool. Lucky me, I gotta metabolism like pissed-off volcano. Even Queen Clozapine and all her slutty daughters barely make me sleepy. Shhh. Don't tell Nurse Happy!

"Aren't you a dear little thing? So conscientious!" Nurse Happy unlocked the meds closet, her big comfortable ass wagglin' in her big comfortable skirt. "A girl like you just makes my day shine a little brighter. One nice person who does what she's told in this pile of devils who'd rather chew off their own tongues—or mine!—than take a silly old pill! But you're not like these brutes, are you, sweet-pea?"

I turned up my blushin' to eleven. "No, Ma'am. I'm sorry being a nurse isn't much fun. I wish it were." I was running out of time. Pretty soon she'd start to see. She'd start to think the blushing wasn't shyness but a weird, scummy sort of excitement. She'd start to think my voice wasn't submissive and soft but making fun of her. She'd feel the black mold snaking in around the edges of me. "If you want, I could take a coupla doses around. To help you out, you know? I like to help. I used to help . . ." I let my dimples come out. Gave her a little nervous giggle, all roses and lace at the edges. *Aw, Ma'am, I'm mostly joshin' ya. I'll still love ya if you say no*.

"Aren't you a dear little thing? What's a girl like you doing in a place like this? Of *course* you can help. Work is good for the soul!" And under her breath she added, "Better you than me." What a peach, Nurse Happy. Oh, don't throw me in the briar patch, Br'er Fox! "Now, you'd better wear this, or they'll get upset. They're like a bunch of old bulls. If they see anything but the white jacket, they start kicking and swinging their horns." She draped a spare orderly's coat over my shoulders. And they say only boys get capes! "Try Mr. Punch over there. He's pretty much on Pluto most of the time. Won't give you any trouble. Probably."

Mr. Punch! What a name! What a guy!

Just like that, I had a Dixie cup grail full of funtime candy in my hot little hand. I got out of there before my five minutes ran down and strolled across the moldy tiles—not too fast, not too fast—to ol' red eyes drooling in a shaft of green-stained sunlight.

"Well, hi there, handsome!" I said.

Our first words! I was all a-flutter!

Mr. Punch's eyes rolled up to meet mine, peering through that screaming yellow hair. Golly wow! It was love at first fright. My boy was burnt all over. Burnt in patterns, burnt on purpose, fulla welts in spirals and angles and dots. And the biggest, prettiest, thickest scars ran down from the corners of his mouth to the bottom of his chin, just where a wooden puppet's mouth would hang open. I love me a burnt man! His bloody eyes burned too, scrapin' over my face, blown pupils snapping in, into focus, into hot, tight, unstoppable *awakeness*. And then he smiled wide and wicked and fanged and needy. Mr. Punch hissed right at me:

"If I had all the wives of wise King Sol, I would kill them all for my Pretty Poll."

That's a quote, that is. Some old-school noise from jolly old London-town. If a man'll rhyme for ya, he'll do just *anything*. From that second, I was Pretty Polly forever and ever amen. I went hot and wet as Mrs. Sarkomand's mermaid cunt all over. My heart had a party dress on. Play it cool, Polly!

"Time for your medication, Mr. Punch," I said softly. But soft wasn't the way to Mr. Punch's hard wooden heart. His pupils melted out again, the arson in his eyes snuffed. He started coughing. His phlegm looked like anybody else's phlegm. Dunno what I expected. Liquid gold or lava or tainted heroin.

"Sorry, Doctor," he slurred. "Thought you were someone else."

I started to tell him not to be such a silly-head. The little girl giggle started in the back of my throat, a fat wad of demureness ready to hack up out of my lungs. But Bad Daddy didn't raise no dumb dolly! Never give up an advantage once you've got it in your briefcase. I brushed some imaginary lint off my white jacket and settled down in the next chaise. Handed Mr. Punch his strings. Open wide, let Doctor Polly see that you swallowed up all your tranq-tastic medicine like a good boy!

Now, I ain't sayin' I'm any great shakes as an actress. But if there's one thing I know, it's how a shrink talks. I can do it all day long. I can do ya Freudian, Jungian, Gestalt, a little Cog-Bee, a little Hypno-whatever, pick a card, any card. Tell me about your mother. What comes to mind when I say the word *match*? I put on my Big Girl voice. Betcha didn't think I had one, huh? Well, fuck you, watch this:

"No trouble at all, Mr. Punch. A growing ability to retain facial awareness from one day to another is an excellent sign of progress. Shall we pick up where we left off?"

"Don' 'member," Mr. Punch warbled as his cocktail kicked in. It was just *sick*, I tell ya, seein' a man like that laid low, blubbin' and stutterin' like he belonged here, like he wasn't a *panther* under that Haldol haze. Like he wasn't a beautiful monster just like me.

"That's perfectly all right. We'll start fresh. The basics. The *root* of the issue." I leaned in close. He smelled like sour sweat and bile and puke—but under that, he smelled like home. "Why are you here, Mr. Punch?"

Mr. Punch's furioso eyes went bloody knifepoints again. I could hear his heart start up insida him like a boiler comin' on in Hell's basement. He grabbed my wrist, dug his nails into me. Don't tell Daddy, but I almost came right there. Mr. Punch snarled one big, black word:

Grimdark.

The word went echoin' round the Pool, down into the deep end and across the bathing beauties of Club Meds. All the other kittens picked it up, tossed it around, gnawed on it, spat it out again. Every wrinkled cock in the place got rage-hard.

Grimdark.

The reason for the season! That big loser ox in body armor who knocked me on the head and dumped me in here. Dumped us all in here. In Sarkomand. In the Pool. In Dr. Leng's Easter basket of bad eggs. Ain't no bunny in the place didn't know that emojock leather-queen fuckmuppet. Oh, wasn't life *grand* in Guignol City before the big fella came along? A girl could burn down City Hall in peace! A boy could really *express* himself artistically—splice his genes with a crocodile's or 'roid out on space-testosterone or just put on a spangled mask and haunt the shadows, followin' his bliss. I grew up in that Guignol. Sure, it's not great for the tax base, but the *culture*, you know? I miss that. I miss the old neighborhoods before Grimdark made the mean streets safe for foreign real estate investment. Now it's like New York after disco hit the skids. Now it's brunch and boutiques and artisanal babies born with a silver EpiPen shoved up their asses. Now this hunka Kevlar and meat-headed super-dickery comes along and decides it's his job to clean up the place. Who asked ya, buddy? Who the shit d'ya think you are? Except no one knows who he is, because of *course* they don't. God, it's just so paint-by-frickin'-numbers. We all hate him—but it's not what you think! We don't hate him for beatin' us or for fightin' for his goody-two-shits section four point zero one of the penal code idea of justice. A nemesis gets your blood goin' in the morning! Archenemies beat coffee every day of the week! Naw, we hate him 'cause he's *boring*.

He's *tortured*. He's *mysterious*. He can bench-press his mommy issues one-handed. He wears all black—not a spangle or a crocodile scale or a measly pop of color in sight. Grimdark isn't *special*—not like Miasma or Doctor Nocturne. He just works out a lot and bought the whole Sharper Image catalog in one go. He's the rich kid in school who whacks ya in the nose and tells the teacher you started it. Well, maybe you did and maybe you didn't, but honestly, Grimdark just likes punchin' things, and that boy was *gagging* for an excuse.

But punching is all he wants to do! All foreplay and no big, final thrust-n-shudder. He's got a Saturday morning cartoon for a moral compass, so he'll beat ya till your kidneys give out and your bones snap like glow sticks, till you'll never look the same again, till a prizefighter's brain scan looks nicer than yours, but he won't *kill* ya. As if noble Mr. Grimdark's somehow in the clear if a fella bleeds out at the hospital, just so long as he didn't actually shoot the poor bastard in the face. For Chrissake, at least Mr. Punch'll putcha out of your misery! But no, he just sticks us all in here, in Sarkomand, because he's such a fantastic genius that tucking all the wickeds of the world in bed together seemed like a super-spiffy idea. That 1% bro-fund manager protein shake addict swoops and swaggers around Guignol City like he owns us all, barfin' up Hallmark-card poems about JUSTICE and REVENGE and DARKNESS along with some seriously freshman poli-sci haiku that sounds super deep and means jack except that a rich man's gonna make a poor man bleed. As if the mutant league of law and order didn't already have the game fixed; now they just don't bother with innocent until proven guilty. These days, it's innocent till we call Grimdark. Listen up: if Meanie Mussolini were kickin' around today, he'd be a superhero. Trust me.

Grimdark.

FUCK THAT GUY. I wanna talk about *me*. This is about me. You have to listen to me! You have to *see* me. I'm smashed in here between Grimdark and Mr. Punch like the world's worst threeway, and yet somehow I never get mine. I pulled off the greatest heist in Guignol City history! I stole Mr. Punch's *attention*. D'ya *know* what it takes to get a supervillain to open up, talk about his feelings, and explore his vulnerability in a safe, healthy environment? It'd be easier to steal the Constitution or burn down Buckingham Palace or whatever boring thing the kids are planning these days. Yeah. It ain't nothin'!

Grimdark.

The red-light district in Mr. Punch's eyes closed up shop again. I felt his forehead, still in Doctor Polly mode. Skin-to-skin contact is very important in establishing a patient bond or some shit. His hair felt like lacquered lightning. Mr. Freud says boys gotta talk about their mama. Mom, Mom, Mom, it's always Mom at the bottom of a rotten soul! But Mr. Ziggy Stardust of the Austrian Amygdala didn't know a damn thing about people like Mr. Punch and me.

"Tell me about your nemesis," I whispered.

Mr. Punch reached one long hand up and stroked the side of my face. It was more like love than anything I'd ever dug outta the bargain bin. It'd been *way* longer than five minutes. And Mr. Punch was still lookin' at me like I was madea marshmallows and he was starvin' to death.

I kept him hopped up pretty good on Klonopin and Haldol and whatever the little pink ones are. Mr. Punch got pink ones and I didn't. Boo. Nurse Happy was delighted to let me take over the candy distribution for the really ugly cases. But after a while, it was just no fun having a Mr. Punch doll who couldn't hardly walk or talk or use his kung-fu grip. Bad Daddy always said I got bored of my toys too easy. Sign of a frivolous brain. But I say toys oughtta step up their game if they wanna stick around! Who can be bothered with the same old dumb dolly day in, day out? Swap out those button eyes for lifelike blinking action and laser-sighting! Stick that plastic pupper down the garbage disposal and gimme a *Good Daddy*.

I palmed the pink ones first.

"Where were you born?" I asked Mr. Punch. I tucked a strand of hair behind my ear. It always looks *très* professional. I am HERE for this business now that I've got that loose hair taken care of!

"Hell," said Mr. Punch. Was that a little less drool? A little smile starting?

"Hell, Florida, or Hell, California?"

Mr. Punch didn't know what to do with that one. It's a good

trick. I always did it with my doctors. Just go along with whatever they say, 'cause they're not about to stop saying it. They hardly even needya there, really. My grumpy ol' patient grunted and flopped his face over to stare at the deep end of the pool, where the Fearwig was busy sharpening a tongue depressor into a shiv with his pincers. Ugh. The Fearwig is gross. He is *never* invited to my birthday party.

"And what year was that, Mr. Punch?"

"1066." The Fearwig shambled over to a fat chick with a tattoo of the world on her dumb face. We watched it happen calmly, with a real sense of companionship, like watching the ocean from a big, white boat deck.

"I have your file, Mr. Punch." I didn't. "You ain't . . . you *aren't* any kind of mystery to me. I already know everything about you. Where you were born and what year doesn't matter. It only matters that you tell me."

Wiggy got his wooden stake up under the heart of the big fat world. Nurse Happy and her crew threw their arms up in the air, wailin' and moanin' like a big-ticket musical, kick-ball-change and shake ya syringes! Jazz hands!

Mr. Punch grinned up at me. *"I'll dance and sing like any thing, with music for my pretty Poll."*

Then he passed clean out. Oh, well.

I swiped the little green pills next. After-dinner mints, I always call 'em.

"At what age did you lose your virginity?" I asked. Was he sittin' up a little straighter? Twitchin' a little less?

"I've known whores and dolls in a hundred halls but I've saved all my love for my pretty Poll."

And he yacked all over the moldy green tiles of old Mrs. Sarkomand's healing natatorium. Aw, Mistah Punch, you can quote at me and puke at me all you want. I want anything that's inside ya. Everything you got.

"What a lovely sentiment, Mr. Punch. But I hardly think that can be true. Even the original Mr. Punch was married to Judy before he met his Pretty Polly." God, but it was hard to keep up that fancy voice! Tasted like Bad Daddy's cigars in my mouth.

Mr. Punch's neon hair gleamed in the watery Pool-light. He kept on talkin' all hunched over where he'd barfed. Like there was a microphone in his slime. "I was twenty-five. I paid a whore to get it over with. She had blond hair and blue eyes, like American girls always do in the movies. Her name was Daisy. When it was done, she said she loved me. Says it to all her johns. That's her calling card, like my strangling men with puppet strings. It's nice to conduct your life with a little flair. I appreciated that about her. She took the time to leave a mark. So, I only broke her hand instead of killing her as I'd planned. Professional courtesy."

Another girl probably woulda stopped there. Who wants to peel back another whack of onion once you hit the hooker-killing slice? Me. I did. People always want me to be good somewhere deep inside, but Bad Daddy was always right about me. I've got shit for a soul and a C-4 heart. So, the next time I got Nurse Happy's white coat on and took that little Dixie sippy cup of meds over to Mr. Punch, I dropped all those pills—the after-dinner mints, the pink ladies, the blue velvets—into my pocket and sat down next to him real close. So close I could smell his emptiness. I looked into his red eyes, the deepest eyes in the whole wide world, deeper'n Hell, Florida, and the Battle of Hastings and all the blood and death that ever happened to anybody ever.

"Tell me your name, Mr. Punch. Your real name."

"I'm no one," he whispered. "It's better to be no one. It's so *lazy* being somebody. Everybody does it. Except *him*. No one knows who *he* is. That's how it should be. No names. Just death in the dark."

I thought long and hard about it. Never give up an advantage. But then again, if you want a boy to like you, you gotta give him presents.

"I know who Grimdark is," I said, cool and casual, like sayin': *I know the name-a that actor in that one show you like*.

Oh, did I not tell ya? I *absolutely* know who Grimdark is. I met him a *buncha* times at Bad Daddy's parties. Practically bounced me on his knee when I was just a wee baby psycho in ribbons and matchsticks. He thinks he's so clever with the black mask and the armor and that fake-ass manly voice, but who is he kidding with that jawline? Please.

Mr. Punch's pupils crackled black and bright. It was him. It was finally *him* in there, and he wanted what I had. I shivered all over. He grabbed my hand. His skin was hot. My heart beat like it could get outta me and jump straight into him.

"Tell me."

"Maybe I will. Maybe I won't," I giggled. He was squeezing my hand so tight, I thought he was gonna break it. Like Daisy the loving hooker. I did get a *little* worried then. You don't get outta Bad Daddy's house without survival instincts. "Maybe it's time for your meds."

He slung on that mad grin. Mr. Punch's patented scars opened and folded into new patterns, deeper patterns. "If you like. They have as much effect on me as the water I take them with, Dr. Ketch. Tell me who he is or I will choke you to death in front of this august audience of Guignol City's greatest hits and has-beens."

"You were *faking*!"

Mr. Punch gave a humble little shrug. *This old thing? How*

sweet of you to notice. I reached out my free hand and stroked the side of his face just like he'd done to me.

"That's all right, sweetie," I crooned. "I was fakin', too. Ain't we a pair?"

I opened Nurse Happy's coat to show the stained green checkered hospital gown inside. I don't think I've seen a thing in this world as nice as the way Mr. Punch looked at me then. Not even my house burning down like justice. He kissed me on the mouth (boy *howdy*, was my baby a good kisser!) and hissed:

"Of all the girls who are so smart, there's none like Pretty Polly. She is the darling of my heart, she is so sweet and jolly!"

It was a cinch and a half to escape. Sometimes, I think they *want* us to get out of Sarkomand and back to good ol' Guignol. If you ever get your situation stuck in there, just shimmy up to the vents in your room. Those old houses got pipes like highways. There's a little spot halfway through the HVAC—you can't miss it. The steel's like a yearbook.

Miasma Was Here.

Doctor Nocturne 2010. 2012. 2015.

See Ya Next Year!

Can't keep a Fat Cat down!

Dr. Leng hopes you've enjoyed your stay. He knows you have many choices when it comes to maximum security incarceration, and thanks you for choosing Sarkomand Sanatorium. Have a Healthy Day!

MEGALODON ROCKS.

Mr. Punch and Pretty Polly Sittin' in a Tree.

I took him to my apartment in Guignol. I knew Daddy wouldn't'a dumped it. Better to let the place sit empty and accumulate equity.

It's expensive to live in the big GC these days! Fuckin' hipsters, man. And you think *I'm* bad.

Funny, Mr. Punch didn't look so scary standin' in my kitchen, wearin' my lime-green kimono like the hottie he was, waitin' for Mr. Coffee to do his thing.

"Tell me," said Mr. Punch.

"Later, Mistah," I laughed. "Whodya think you're talkin' to? This is a straight-up Scheherazade situation we got here. If I spill those beautiful black beans, whaddo I got? A big fat nothin'. I wanna be *involved*, Mr. Puppet Man. I wanna be your girl. So, just you play tea party with me like a good dolly and maybe I'll give you your treat."

And that's how I kept my man. He was my dog on a leash and the leash was a name I couldn't say till I knew I'd be safe. Till I could make him a Good Daddy.

It was like college, livin' with Mr. Punch! We slept all day and ran wild at night. My sweet baby boo burned my face just like his! We used coat hangers heated up in the gas oven, and after, we went straight out and burned down the Harlequin Theater together—how very dare they put on the same lazy sack of mayonnaise-plays every couple of years? We saved the world from another goddamned *Romeo and Juliet*, I tell ya. It was *charity*. We robbed the Guignol City Bank and Trust, we killed up the board of trustees of Guignol Electric and Power in one glorious night of monologues and machine-gun fire. We kidnapped a gaggle-a grad students and made 'em cook up a rapid-release water-soluble hallucinogen in my little kitchen. We were just a couple of wacky kids in love! And in between he'd fuck me on the floor of my flat and ask me over and over. Beg me. *Tell me his name, you bitch. You cunt. I love you. I'll always love you, Pretty Polly, you dumb fucking whore, you stupid bag of meat, tell me his name. I love you so, I love you so, I'll never leave you, no, no, no.* He choked me for funsies and it felt like a warm glass of milk at bedtime. He called me a cunt and it sounded like *darling*.

Well, okay, he didn't *fuck* me, exactly. No matter what we did, nothing really happened down south. But Mr. Punch wouldn't leave his girlie hangin', no sir! He had a wooden thingy he tied on with puppet strings. It was painted all over with Death and the Devil and the Judge and all the rest of the kittens in your average Punch and Judy show. And with that thing strapped on, he did me proud. I don't mind. We're all broken somehow.

I'll tell ya, I was feeling pretty good about life on Planet Me. We had plans for the future, Mr. Punch and me! My sweetie supported *my* dreams. He said any time I wanna go drown Bad Daddy in gasoline, he'd make me a packed lunch with a prize inside! He was gonna fix me up a cozy li'l nest in the police commissioner's mansion, bread in the pantry and booze in the fridge. And something BIG in the oven. Mr. Punch and Pretty Polly were gonna reel in the big fish. Stop runnin' from the big lunk in the black mask and take our city back. Mr. Punch had a plan.

"We'll go to him. You and me, my darling dunce. My Pretty Poll, my candy cunt. Hunt him down in his own bed. We'll dress up for the New Year masquerade—you know how I love a mask at midnight! He'll be there. Everyone in Guignol who matters will be there! They'll simper and dance and tell each other how wonderful they are for dumping their caviar at a shelter after they're done slurping it up. At midnight, we won't mess about with any sort of SWAT team nonsense or security system tampering. I shall simply walk up to him, curl my arm round his waist, and slip a knife into his heart. As intimate and quiet as a divorce. And all I need, my

Pretty Poll, my rotting angel, my heart, my numbskull nymphet, is his name. Then we will be free and together until the heat death of Guignol City, which I expect to follow shortly."

So I told him. Why not? He loved me. I loved him. All that crap about Scheherazade was in the past. Love is love! Nothin' can get past love. So I told him. I lay my head on his chest and breathed in his smell and gave up the goods.

"Glenn Falk. Glenn Falk is Grimdark."

Golly, but Mr. Punch fucked me then! His flesh and my flesh, warm and alive and *matching*. Matching scars, matching teeth, matching eyes. He fucked me for real, without the marotte. That's what it's called. His puppet stick. See, I know things. I know lots of things. I went to Harvard, you judgmental bitches. Suck my Crimson Tide. Mr. Punch came inside me like a war crime. We broke the bed! *We'll laugh about this tomorrow and steal a new one*, I thought.

Afterward, he drowned me in the bathtub.

There was a moment, just before I gave up and breathed in all that dirty, soapy, passion fruit bubble bath–scented death, where I thought I had it wrong. Maybe that day in Sarkomand when Mr. Punch said, *I thought you were someone else*, he'd meant: *I thought you were a crippled baby antelope I could chase down across the veldt and pick the lock to this place with your bones*. Maybe I was just a funny little clown in the Punch and Grimdark show. Maybe he never once meant *I love you* when he called me a cunt, he just meant that I was a stupid, useless, disgusting hole he hated only slightly less than himself. What if we were never any little bit alike, except that we wanted to burn the awful old world down? But it was just barely possible that I was the only one who cared *what* world we blew up. The world of rich men playing in costumes and electric companies turning on the dark everywhere they went and shithead greaseheart daddies all the way down—that was my tune. Maybe my baby was just trying to fuck his way through me and the bed and the floor and the city to get to *him*. Maybe Mr. Punch was a Bad Daddy, after all.

NAW.

I'm just foolin'! No frickin' way! My boo is true blue! It was just a game! Everything's a game with Mr. Punch! He's comin' *back* for me. I'm not like you blubbering cows. *My* man's gonna come through. He's not gonna forget about me, no siree! He'll pull out the Fearwig's teeth one by one till he gives up the formula for de-corpsifying my hot little ass and then we'll paint the town RED. Hell, once we've got the goods, he can drown me or choke me or drop me off a building any time he wants and snatch me back for breakfast! It'll be the most fun we can have with our clothes on! Don't you worry about me, chickadees.

Any minute, you'll see. Mr. Punch is gonna grab onta me and never let go.

THE HELL HATH CLUB VS. THE MIGHT OF ATLANTIS

All eyes turn to the lady in green. She swirls a spoon around her coffee cup. It doesn't make any noise. Thank the tiny baby Jesus, down here in Deadtown we are spared the constant tinkle of silverware against porcelain that plagues the restaurant industry. A long, long red curl slides out of the black pearl comb in her hair and lands on the table like a spurt of blood. It hurts to look at it. Like a camera flashing in your eyes. The sides of her head are shaved down to red fuzz, just the one long horsetail left, running up and over and down her spine like a special-edition collect-them-all punk-rock Barbie doll. She doesn't notice us staring. I love my girl Bayou to a hundred million pieces, but she's like one of those thorny old fish who hide on the seafloor, totally still and silent, blending in, waiting for something tasty to drift on by.

Only she doesn't blend in. Not for a second. It's hard to blend in when your skin is covered in green crystal scales. When you look like a torch singer who stayed on stage so long, she chemically bonded with her costume. She never wants to talk. *I'll go tomorrow*, she always says, but she never does. *I talked yesterday*. But she didn't. Never jam today, that's Miss B to a T.

Miss B suddenly notices no one's talking. She blushes, which looks weird on a green girl. Like Christmas lights. "Oh! Can I get anyone another coffee? Tea? I think Neil's hiding some wine back there under his wings. I saw it. Pinot and Cab and some black dusty stuff with a Greek name."

Neil shrugs behind the counter. He tucks his lolling gargoyle tongue back behind his fangs the way that classy old guys smooth their neckties or clean their glasses. Reaches under one great big bat-wing and produces a bottle wrapped in black straw. Sidles on over with a tray of glasses, holds the cork for Bayou to sniff. She nods; he pours. Rich emptiness glugs into each of our glasses—the living will *never* let a decent wine grape go extinct. But the Bordeaux tumbles out for her, thick and red and reeking of fruit and sunlight and dirt and stone. We all stare while she drinks it. We watch her throat move. I'm not saying it's not creepy. It totally is. But we can't stop. She's so *bright*. I never kissed a girl when I was alive, but death has a way of loosening your inhibitions.

"Your turn, Queen B," I say. I want to touch her hand but I don't. She can touch me but I can't touch her. Them's the rules here in the strip club of the damned.

"Oh, no, I don't have anything to say. I'll go tomorrow. What about Daisy? Or Sam? Please. Don't worry about me. I'm not . . . It's not my place. It's not right. I'm not like you.

"I'm not single.

"I'm not human.

"I'm not dead.

"Deadtown is just my summer home. My Hamptons. My Riviera. Every year, I drive up to the old black house, fire up the boiler, dust the tables and chairs, scrub the windows, stock the larder with apples and cereal and grief, try to find something good on the radio."

She runs one glittering green finger around the rim of her

wineglass. The wine shivers and grows crosshatches like a speaker. A wet crackle shimmies up out of the gargoyle's personal stash: *Welcome to DPR, Deadtown Public Radio, the Voice of the Underworld. This afternoon on All Things Cadaverous: Ada Lovelace and Grace Hopper address the issues surrounding piracy and VPN access in the city center . . .*

"So, you see, it's not fair for me to take time from all of you. At the end of the summer, I'll go home like always. There's a place down by the docks, a little way along the boardwalk. I'll walk there and buy an ice cream cone and when I finish it, I'll dive off the pier and swim down to the bottom of everything, past the rusted bicycles and six-pack rings and anglerfish and oil drums until I find the little golden grate that leads back to the land of the living. It's been in my family for centuries. My grandfather hired a gargoyle to guard it. He's all gills and spines and baleen. Still keeps the buttons on his uniform bright, even in the briny deep. I'll bring him a bottle of whiskey and kiss his cheek as I swim by. *Say hello to your family for me, Mort*, I'll whisper. And he'll bow. And in a year, I'll do it all over again. Unless I find him this time."

"Find who?" Hazel asks.

"My son. He has to be here somewhere. He *is* here. Deadtown is a big place, maybe the biggest place, but I'm actually a very organized person. The city is a grid. I search quadrant by quadrant. And someday I'll see him, swinging on a tire in a park or peering into the windows of an automat or splashing in a fire hydrant. Maybe he's living with other dead children in some blackstone with brown ivy over the door. It doesn't matter where he is. I'll find him and the world will stop being a terrible place and everything will go back to the way it was when I was young."

Samantha reaches out for the lady in green but stops short. Her hand hovers over Bayou's shoulder, squeezing empty air. "Sweetheart, it's time. You won't go tomorrow. You didn't go yesterday. Time to pay your dues to the Hell Hath Club."

Bayou takes a deep breath and straightens her shoulders. Something comes into her eyes. Something hungry and young and manic. Something a lot less elegant. Something a lot less serene than little Miss Oh-Don't-Worry-About-Me.

"All right. Okay. How do you start? John used to go to AA. So, I guess I could do the HH version. So, yeah. Okay. My name is Bayou, Trash Queen of Backwater Atlantis, Alligator Princess of the Great Galactic Delta, the Creature from the Rhinestone Lagoon, and I hate my husband."

THE BALLAD OF BLUE BAYOU

I never wanted children. Let's get that straight up top. All I ever wanted to do was to drink beer, play my horn, and ride mutant armadillos till the end of the world. But you don't get to hit those high notes when you're Queen of something. Hard to scream-sing *fuck the man authority is deathpuke anarchy in Atlantis* when your mom is, like, the *entire* government.

I know what you've heard about Atlantis. But it's not what you think. There's no perfect crystal towers, no vending machines packed with enlightenment in a can, no visions of techno-utopian sugarplums dancing in the streets. Atlantis does not have ancient wisdom in every pot or a golden submarine in every garage. It's just a city that happens to be underwater. Like most cities, it's got some good neighborhoods, a couple of cool clubs, a butcher, a baker, a candlestick maker, and the rest is pretty much a shithole. You think of an underwater city and your brain spins up all these postcards of clean turquoise water and whitecaps and frolicking orcas off a Lisa Frank notebook. But the ocean isn't like that. It's full of salt and sewage and tanker oil and mud and dead dolphins and fish poop and about a billion and four jellyfish. We don't live in Atlantis because it's a pristine paradise. We live there because we're weird, gross aliens and Brooklyn's full. Plus, for us? Breathing air is like knocking back shots of whiskey. The longer we do it, the loopier and punchier and louder and dizzier we get until eventually we pass out in a toilet or die. A fresh summer breeze will get an Atlantean shit-faced drunk.

I told you. I'm not human. I'm not a goddamned mermaid, either, so don't get any ideas about shell-bras or selling my voice to a sea-witch. That little idiot deserved to die. Never give up your voice for a man, you fucking *guppy*. Atlanteans are sort of . . . half alligator, half siren, half electric eel. Yes, I know that's three halves. Don't get any of your slimy binary brain on me. We came from another planet or another dimension or some woo-woo place. I never could keep it straight. Who cares how we got here? This is where we live *now*. The Dumbfuck Dimension obviously doesn't miss us. Even though they *should*, because we're *gorgeous* and we live for ages and we're all psychic and really kick ass at water polo. Any ecosystem would be lucky to have us.

And among the weird, gross alligator-eel aliens, I'm royalty. It's not my fault. I didn't ask to be born to the Fascist Bitch-Queen Delphine Tankerbane the Fourth. If I could've picked, I'd have been born like my friend Platypunk—out in the backwater boondocks to a hairdresser and a bartender, living in a trailer park hacked out of a fossilized Portuguese man o' war, smoking brain coral and being awesome. But nobody picks. I swam off from the palace as soon as possible.

I call it a palace. It's basically like if you built a Jenga tower out of shipwrecks. Mom's got a little of all of them in there. Captain's cabins from the *Mary Celeste* and the *Flying Dutchman* and the *Lusitania*—you would not *believe* how much crap she lifted off the *Titanic* before humans started shining searchlights on the thing and diving for rust. Aw, you still don't get it. Think big. She swiped

an *entire ballroom* for the royal chamber. Her throne is made out of a thousand silver teapots with WHITE STAR LINE stamped on them. It's all just garbage. Junk. How come I was the only one who could see that? I hightailed it the second Mumsy wasn't looking. Out into the *real* city. Into the muck and the noise, down to Squid Row where no one cares who you are, to Soho where everyone's furious and starving and beautiful, into the East Gillage, swarming with throbbing techno whale song, snarling skinny punks with fish-hooks in their ears, angler-headed hipsters burning for the ancient undersea connection to that salty dynamo in the machinery of the deep.

That's where I met Platypunk. I don't know what his deal was, taxonomically speaking. He had sleek, soft fur like an otter instead of scales like me, poisonous barbs on his heels, webbed feet, a hot pink mohawk, and claws for days. We started a band. Blowhole? Maybe you've heard of us? Platy sang and played the lionfish; I was on drums and conch. I bet you think conches just sort of bleat out one non-note, don't you? No way. Not when an Atlantean is on the horn. My conch did whatever I told it to. Scream or whisper, whistle nice or empty the room. We played all the hot stages in Atlantis, him and me. Sometimes I close my eyes and pretend we're still bringing the house down at Sea Bee's, right at that part in "Anarchy in Atlantis" where Platy just starts quacking like a maniac at the top of his lungs, and then we both jump into the crowd and they carry us away in their arms and everything is good forever.

Point is, I was happy before John Heron came along. I was *fine*. I was *myself*. Every story I told was about me. I was better than a punk. I was a *protagonist*. No kids, no husband, no throne. No problems. No clawing sense of loss the color of the sea's guts. No dead mother. No dead son. I didn't even know what it felt like to have a shark chew my leg off! Good times. The best times.

So, this is how it happened. Strap in, because this is about the lamest part of my whole soggy joke of a life. Falling in love is embarrassing. It is not hardcore. It is not part of the scene.

I was sort of half–shacked up with this guy named Crowjack at the time. He had a swim-up apartment in the Gillage, wrote plays full of halibut whinging about their fathers and the pressures of masculinity. After the show, his or mine, we'd all go down to Platypunk's dad's bar, the Great White Whaler, and do some blow. Free pints of sour beer with shot glasses full of real topside air dropped in. Platypunk Sr. always had great air. Kept it in a couple of scuba tanks behind the bar. You had to be in the know to get any, know the handshake, that sort of thing. I was a hard drinker back then. Part of the uniform. A little oxy, a whiff of nitro, pound that garbage beer, lick a shaker of ozone off my wrist, throw back a shot of smog and suck a slice of seaweed to take the edge off. But Crowjack *loved* to drink. He had his own tank and mask at home, and half the days, he'd just float on the current that flowed between the bedroom and the kitchen with his mask on, sucking down oxy until he thought he was God. Platypunk always said he was a douche bag and I guess he was right.

"Hey, baby Bayou. Let's get outta here," Crowjack slurred at us Upon That Fateful Night. "Let's go somewhere we can *really* get wrecked. Where they've got the good stuff, on tap, none of these canned farts."

I was feeling good. Scratch that. I was feeling fucking *spectacular*. Blowhole had hauled our first full house that night. Two separate fistfights broke out during the bridge of "I Wanna Be Mutated," which is how you spell a truly epic show. I should've known what he meant, but I was feeling too nice to do my usual trick of sifting through everything Crowjack said in case there was something fucked up floating around in there.

"Naw, man," said Platypunk. "I don't do that shit. It's hardcore, balls-to-the-wall *boring*. You shouldn't either, Miss B. We got lunch with the guys from Oily Penguin tomorrow. Besides, your mom would *kill* you if she found out."

When you think about it, it's all Platypunk's fault. The number one bull's-eye easiest-peasiest way to make sure I'll do something is to tell me how it would piss off my mother. So, Crowjack and I blew out of the Great White Whaler like a couple of speedboats and started the long swim up to the surface. Because of *course* that's what he meant. That's where you get the strongest air. Where it gets you—and all for free. I couldn't believe how warm the water was that close to land. How blue. How clear. It felt like hot velvet diamonds rolling over my skin. Our heads busted up out of a wave into a liquid gold-red twilight and a wind like cocaine-moonshine. Crowjack just huffed it all in. His pupils blew out so big and black! He threw himself backward against the next wave, giggling and paddling around like a kid. It didn't hit me quite as hard. I took shallow breaths—too much to swallow all at once. I looked at the sun instead. My first sunset, sinking in the sky like a goldfish on fire. I looked at my skin in the light of the breathing world, glittering like a disco ball where the sun bounced and jangled off me. Off in the distance I saw an island with nothing on it but a tower with a light on top of it. Below the tower, people moved. I could see their shadows on the long grass.

People. Others. Humans.

"I wanna go home," I whispered to Crowjack. "I feel sick."

And I did. I ducked under the whitecaps for a minute to get my head on straight.

"What are you talking about? We just got here! I'm not even buzzed yet."

I rolled my eyes. "Yes, you are, dumbass. You're such a lightweight."

I was only teasing. But you can't tease anybody who writes plays about their father. Crowjack hauled off and punched me in the eye. Punched! Not slapped. Closed-fist. Like he meant it. Like he'd been holding that in. Well, fuck that for nothing. Bye, bye, Crowjack. I wasn't in love with him anymore, anyway. He cried almost every time we had sex. And I was a far better swimmer. With a couple of kicks, I got well away from that cliché little scene. A couple more and I could hardly see him. Only a little shape in the waves, flailing his arms and yelling that he was sorry. Who cares, lightweight? I might like a bruise or two in good fun—I look tough as hell with bruises. But back then, I didn't take that action from anybody. I swam and swam, ducking down below and popping up again, feeling my strength, feeling my speed. I was pretty hammered by then, I admit. I wasn't paying attention. I got too close to the island. One of those people-shadows saw me and stopped moving around. Then, for absolutely no goddamned reason, it jumped into the water and started swimming after me! I should have just gone down bubble, but I was too shocked and drunk to move. The shadow turned out to be a man, a big, nice-looking man with a good beard and thick hair the color of the sun. He grabbed me around the neck and started hauling me to shore.

"It's okay!" the man yelled back. "I got you! You're gonna be fine!"

"What? Stop! Hold on!" I coughed and spluttered. The way he was dragging me, I kept getting wind up my nose.

"Good thing I saw you! I thought you were driftwood for a

minute," he went on, panting with the effort of saving me. "Or a seal. But better safe than sorry! You almost drowned!"

"This is ridiculous," I snarled, and squirmed out of his grip in one quick duck-and-twist. "I don't need your help! Do I *look* like I need your help?"

I don't believe John Heron really saw me before that moment. He was in Burly Savior Noble Guardian of Life mode when he grabbed me. All he saw was a girl in the water. But he sure saw me then. Six long feet of green crystal scales and blue switchblade-fins and really almost pornographically suggestive gills and bruised cheekbone and half-shaved-off red hair. But I saw him, too. He had the warmest green eyes and the kindest way of holding his mouth, even when he was dumbfounded and gawking like a damn fool. Those muscles didn't hurt, either, even if they were a weird brownish color. He was handsome as hell, and most importantly, he didn't look like anyone I'd ever met in my life. He looked *new*. We treaded water in total silence for, well, god knows how long. Finally, he said:

"Are you a mermaid?"

"That's racist," I snapped. My head was starting to spin. Crowjack was right. The air was amazing up there.

He backpedaled immediately. "I'm sorry! I didn't mean it; I don't . . . What happened to your eye?"

"Bad boyfriend," I answered, and touched my face. Still tender.

Then it happened. I couldn't help it. I laughed in this weird way that had nothing to do with me, this soft, coquettish, flirty laugh like a fucking sea lion in heat. Gross. It's the air, you know. Everything that came after, I blame on that stone-cold bitch oxygen. She hates me and wants me to suffer. I loved him. I loved him like breathing. I loved him *because* I was breathing. I was reeling on the whiskey-wind, my vision gone to oil and honey as I pounded shot after shot of pure unfiltered sky.

We screwed under the stars on the beach below his lighthouse. It wasn't very good for me. He didn't vibrate the water with his legs to signal his interest. His torso didn't flush that delicate shade of blue that really gets me going. He didn't clack his swim bladders against each other to make the secret song of Atlantean sex. He didn't even have claspers or a cloaca. We had to do it his way. It took *forever*. But it certainly was new. I straddled him and clacked my swim bladders deep in my throat and I could feel the blue coming on in my chest, lighting up his dumb handsome face with the light of another dimension. Afterward, we swam out together so I could sober up. He told me about himself. He was an orphan, found screaming on the shore by Angus Heron, the old man who ran the lighthouse, and raised to keep that light on like it could save the world. It was romantic. Like a fairy tale. Like a song written by someone other than me. I told him about my music. Sang him a bit of "Lemuria Calling."

"I have a secret," he said, floating in the shallows, little harmless green jellyfish glowing along the strand like stage lights.

"Don't we all?"

"I want to tell you mine." He looked at me intensely, through his long wet gold hair. He looked at me like I was the answer at the back of a math book. "I . . . I can talk to fish. Not just fish. Dolphins and whales and seals and eels and scallops and crabs. I can talk to them, and when they talk back, I understand everything they say."

I laughed. "So? Who can't?"

John looked hurt. He actually blushed. "Well, pretty much everybody on the planet but me, actually. The truth is, I'm . . . I'm a superhero. People call me Avast." I crooked one crystal, scaly eyebrow. "I fight . . . you know . . . injustice and villainy. I'm part of a group. The Union. With a bunch of other guys. Kid Mercury, Grimdark, the Insomniac, the Unstoppable Id, Chiaroscuro."

I crossed my arms over my chest. I didn't care about any of those stupid names. They sounded like particularly shitty scene bands. "*I'm* on the planet, John."

But he was still in a huff because I wasn't impressed by his little party trick. "*On* the planet. Not under it."

"That's such a mammalian thing to say," I sighed. "'The planet' is seventy percent water, you know."

John's face broke apart. He gave in. He cared that much what I thought. "I know, I know. I'm sorry. Please don't be mad."

I rolled my eyes. "You can talk to fish. Fine. Can you breathe underwater? Or at least hold your breath for a really long time?"

Slowly, John Heron nodded. I narrowed my eyes. My catch of the day was starting to smell suspicious.

"How old are you?"

This was clearly the big one. He didn't want to say. John couldn't look at me and talk at the same time. He fiddled with some invisible thing in the water. "About . . . about eighty-five?"

He didn't look a day out of college.

"Let me see your feet," I sighed. But I already knew. *You have got to be kidding me. What are the fucking chances?*

I hadn't noticed before. I know we had sex and everything, but I'm not really into feet that way. I checked under his arms and under his hair. John Heron, alleged human male, had webbed toes, gills, and tiny vestigial skull-fins the color of the jellyfish on the beach.

"Mystery solved," I purred in his ear. "You're one of us. Half one of us, anyway. Welcome to Freak City. Watch out—it gets real stupid here."

• • •

And indeed it did get real stupid, real fast.

I shouldn't have gotten knocked up. It's so easy when you're doing it with other fish! If it's not mating season, I'm not releasing eggs and it's all good times and kippers for breakfast after. But John's got a lot of mammal in him, and I guess the rules are different. Probably what happened to his poor mother, whoever she was. Girl thought she was going topside for a bit of blow and strange and all of a sudden—*BAM*. Egged up something terrible. Atlantean girls go from zero to mum in about six weeks, so I just . . . stuck around. I couldn't face my mother or Platypunk or Crowjack. I couldn't face being on stage screaming out "Atlantean Idiot" with a big ol' baby belly. It is the *opposite* of punk rock.

The best part of giving birth was the look on John Heron's face. I don't know what he saw in his sex-ed filmstrips, but I'm pretty sure it wasn't a green girl squatting in the ocean in broad daylight while she pushes out an aquamarine egg the size of a dinghy and tries to hide what's happening from the kids in their floaties and swim trunks. He thought the daddy's job was to smoke a cigar and change a couple of diapers, not to wait until nightfall to drag the egg onto the sand and secrete a nutritive acid from his eyes to dissolve the shell. I don't think I ever loved him again as much as I did while he wept over our son, fire-colored gunk hissing and popping on the eggshell, laughing at the total bugfuck absurdity of what was happening to him. When the glassy blue egg had half-melted away, I reached my arms down into the last of the glittering yolk. I felt tiny fingers clutch my hand.

Look, I have never been anything but hardcore since I said my first swear, but when my son grabbed onto me for the first time, it was like a harpoon in the heart. Nothing ever hurt so much or felt so good. I lifted him out of the egg and held him in my arms. He didn't cry. He held on to my hair in his fists.

Of course, he wasn't *him* yet. Atlanteans are born hermaphroditic, telepathic, about as far along as a human two-year-old, and completely transparent. We pigment up over childhood. In kindergarten, most of us still have clear patches all over. I counted diamond ribs through crystal skin.

"It'll be a boy in about a year," I whispered to John.

We both stared at our child. I was amazed any creature could be so perfect and beautiful. John was amazed that his kid looked like a glass Christmas ornament of the baby Jesus.

We named him Angus. John insisted, after his foster father. I only gave in because everything else about Angus was all me. You'd never know he had any mammal in the mix at all. When he cried, it sounded like whale song. But when we were alone I called him Azure. A proper pedigreed Atlantean name for the secret prince of the sea. Because I still hadn't told John who I was. Who my mother was. I liked just being Bayou for somebody in the world. Just being loved. But after Angus was born, we had to go home. Hatchlings just can't live on land. It'd be like filling a baby's bottle full of rum and cramming it up his nose all day. A growing boy needs salt water.

This is the part you've been waiting for. I know what stories fill the seats, and it's not the one about the punk rock alligator princess getting knocked up. That's what happens *before* the real story. Or offstage during an act break. Babies just sort of happen to heroes at random moments, like a new superpower, and then they're off to the *real* excitement. But Angus and I happened to each other. Lucky accidents. All the way down, his gentle little voice spoke in my head, and my rough, air-shredded whiskey-whisper murmured in his. I kept looking over at John, swimming so beautifully, like he'd never walked in his life, wondering if he could hear us. But I guess he was too human for that.

Mama, what are those?

Those are orcas, Azure. We'll sneak out while Daddy's sleeping and play hide-and-seek with them, just you wait.

Mama, why is the ocean blue?

Because blue is the color of love, my darling. Everything good is blue.

We glided up the long road to the palace, and for once, it looked wonderful to me, in all its rusted trash-heap glory. I was going to present my mother with her first grandchild, with the chorus to a song I hadn't even known I was playing, with the future. I flushed pink with pride. *She'll love you*, I told John, though it was even money she'd hate him. *Don't be nervous. You're coming home. Atlantis never turns away her own. Maybe we'll even find your parents. One of them, anyway. You look kind of like this girl I know who plays the drums in Zombie Starfish and the Great Pacific Garbage Patch.*

But the doors of the palace were shut. Not just shut, barricaded with the masts of the *Flying Dutchman* and the *Mary Celeste*. Not just barricaded but guarded by two burly Atlanteans, a giant squid with anger issues, and a great white shark. Not just shut and barricaded and guarded but sporting a big sign with scrawly, terrible penmanship:

COMMONERS KEEP OUT BY ORDER OF MEGALODON

(AND ALSO BAYOU WHO CAN FUCK RIGHT OFF)

Six weeks is a long time to be gone, I guess. All the clubs had shut down till further notice. Platypunk and his family had gone into hiding. No one had any plankton and no one had any hope and no one had any idea what the hell was going on. Half the royal family was in lockup—Davy Jones's Memorial Hospital for the Violent and Insane. And some asshole named Megalodon ruled Atlantis with an iron fin. But no one had seen the boss himself, only his muscle. So, what did we do? We did what anyone would do when they're young and in love and looking after their first baby.

We beat the shit out of a shark.

It felt good to fight side by side. People always forget that we did. Anything he can do, I can do upside down and holding a baby in one arm. He was only ever half-Atlantean. I am a full-size candy bar. I laid out one of the guards with a barroom dirty kick, then tied the 'roided-out squid's tentacles together in a big party bow. I looked over and John had crushed the other guard's green skull with his fist and was riding the shark like a mechanical bull, banging the poor fella into Megalodon's sign. Into the word BAYOU. Over and over until the great white passed out cold and the barricade buckled.

Inside. Down the long hall of the *Bismarck*'s hull. My home. I was born there. I was made of glass there. And from the *Bismarck* into the *Titanic*'s tenth ballroom, to my mother's silver-teapot throne. On one side of the thing, Platypunk crouched miserably in a cage with a marine research tracking collar around his neck, chained to the floor. On the other, my mother, Delphine Tankerbane the Fourth, lay flat on her face, her beautiful hair trailing up behind her, collared and leashed at the neck, the wrists, the ankles, with her blood floating around her like a black jellyfish. Too much blood. Too much blood for this to be a dream I could wake up from and have my mom call me BeeBee and snuggle me like she did when I was a little glass guppy and we'd never had a single fight and I didn't even know how to play the conch yet.

On the throne sat Crowjack.

Only he wasn't Crowjack anymore. Not completely. His legs had fused into a thrashing thick tail. His emerald-plated head was almost fully transformed into the maw and dead eyes of a prehistoric shark. He snapped his massive rows of teeth. When he saw me, his suddenly broad, powerful chest began to glow electric blue. The blue of love. The blue of mating.

"Crowjack! What the fuck? What did you do?"

"I found it, Bayou! I found a way back home. To our own dimension. This is what we're supposed to look like! This is what we *are*! The greatest predators in any ocean in the universe! It feels amazing. It feels *right*. It's your stupid mother and all the fish-gut aristocrats who keep us trapped in miserable half-primate bodies! I'll show you. I'll show you the way. The sea . . . is full of doors, Bayou. And all the doors lead to power. And what the shit is that thing you dragged back?"

"Call me Avast, cruel villain!" John cried. "Wherever injustice rears its hideous head, wherever tyranny casts its baleful gaze, wherever evil sails the sea, there you will find Avast ready and able to strike it down!"

Megalodon blinked. I gawked at my husband. "Is this a joke?" snarled the shark-thing on the throne. "What are you talking about? Sit down, Shakespeare; this is between me and my little princess."

"The lady is mine," Avast growled. It was like we'd gotten zapped into one of Crowjack's shitty performance pieces, throwing around purple prose and noble angst like beach balls.

I didn't even get a chance to say I wasn't either of theirs. Crowjack wasn't stupid. He saw a child in my arm and a stranger at my side and suddenly I didn't exist anymore. Just his rage. Avast's righteousness. It wasn't about me anymore and it never would be again. It was about halibut and fatherhood and the pressures of masculinity. Megalodon lunged at us and we fought him, and I suppose if you could have sat up in a balcony seat, there would have been some elegance to the fight, some beauty. Fighting can be like that, sometimes. Megalodon yelled out lines from his own terrible plays and Avast bellowed about justice and freedom in a way that made me seriously question my romantic choices and I stayed grimly silent, clutching my son to me, swinging wild, aiming for my ex-boyfriend's eyes.

I should have found a place for Angus to hide. I should have put him down. It all happened so fast. I thought I could protect him. And one moment it all seemed to be going so well, and in another Megalodon shrieked beyond human hearing and turned on me, snatching my glass boy from my arms and swallowing him whole. Angus's voice went out in my head like a blown pilot light. *Mama, mama, it's so loud*—and then nothing. The emerald dinosaur freak sitting in my mother's chair laughed at me. He laughed, and laughed, and laughed, then spun round, bit off Avast's arm, and swam through the ceiling into the dark water, screaming *Avast Avast Avast* like a curse, like a need, like a promise, like the reverb fading out at the end of a furious song.

Oh, the arm grew back. We're like starfish; it's a thing we can do. And it all went on like you've heard, Avast and Megalodon, their endless undersea boxing match. Submarines full of other men, Union men, with masks and costumes and hard-set jaws. Oaths to fight to the death, to never yield, to never surrender, to never stop. But in all those oaths and boasts and proclamations of might and right, Avast never said our son's name. Oh, yes, he would have vengeance, but for "my son." As though I didn't exist. As though Angus, as though *Azure* was nothing but a stolen painting or a bloody nose. A blow to Avast's pride.

All I felt was nothing. I could fight as well as any of them. And I did. Up there, he's a superhero. Down here, I'm Queen of Atlantis. I command the seas. You can call me a sellout if you want. I deserve it. Platypunk did. He tried to get me to run off with him to the Indian Ocean where none of this absurdity could find us, and I said no. What was I supposed to do? My family was dead. Atlantis was well and truly fucked. I told myself it was just another stage. Just another costume. But I knew the truth. Punk dies the day the mortgage comes due. I slipped out of my sturgeon-skin coat and fishhook earrings and into my mother's pale green glam gown of glitter and responsibility. I let them put the Abalone Crown on my head. But I wouldn't grow my hair out. Never. They couldn't make me.

God, I made all the Union boys so uncomfortable. I got in between them and the mirror they liked to preen in, the mirror that showed them all as Kings of the Known Universe. They all felt safe with their girlfriends' ambitions—artists and actresses and scientists. Girls you could brag to the alumni magazine about, but no one they ever had to compete with. They were the sparkly shiny special ones in their houses. After all, science is great, but who can compete with superpowers?

Well, the Queen of Atlantis can.

To tell you the truth, Avast hated Atlantis. Up there, he was a hero. He was totally unique, from New York to New Delhi. Down here, with me, he was just like everyone else. He got so angry at me, over nothing, over everything, over having to spend another second in a place where no one cared that he could tell a whale what to do, where no one knew he was a star. He never touched me anymore. If he came home and saw my chest light up with blue at the sight of him, his lip curled up in disgust and he buried himself in his workouts.

They never once asked me to join their little club. Even after Megalodon opened the floodgates and half a dimension's worth of our redneck cousins poured through. Even after I defeated Whitewater and the Werekraken in the Battle of the Bermuda Triangle. Megalodon only barely escaped that one. He holed up in Guignol City like a trust fund baby for months after, licking his wounds. Even then, my husband and his friends never said, *Hey, you're pretty handy; wanna learn the secret handshake?* And fucking *hell*, they hated my crying at night. *I* hated my crying at night. But I couldn't help it, could I? John Heron never heard Angus's little voice in his head. His father was still puttering around, replacing lightbulbs in his cozy little house. Easy come, easy go. They hated hearing the word *baby. Child.* It messed up the blocking of their play about themselves. Avast could scream, *I shall destroy you for the death of my son!* and his boys would all cheer. But if I so much as touched my stomach and whispered that I missed my baby, oh, how they'd sneer!

I did everything I was supposed to do. I ruled a nation and battled the forces of aquatic evil. Wherever injustice reared its hideous head, wherever tyranny cast its baleful gaze, wherever evil sailed the sea, I showed up to work and punched my card. But still they whispered about me. In the grottos, in the shallows where they could all breathe easy after dinner, half off their faces on my mother's sixty-year squid-ink scotch.

"I think she's losing it," Kid Mercury said.

"She's definitely not normal," Grimdark piled on. "Honestly, Johnny, the kid was barely a week old. It's not like she can't have another one. Maybe you should start trying again."

Chiaroscuro shook his head. So concerned! "Who knows what could happen if . . . if someone like her really went totally mentally *airborne*. The veils between the Atlantean dimensions look like someone's grotty old underwear as it is."

"I don't know. Just let her be, man," sighed the Insomniac, but no one paid any attention to him. Thanks, superheroes! You've truly saved the day! What would the world do without you?

John Heron, Avast, my husband, my golden lighthouse in the dark, my fire-weeping darling, slugged back the last of a scotch my mother had been saving for her jubilee and groaned. "I wish I'd never met her. I know that's a horrible thing to say. I'd never tell her, not in a hundred years. But god, whenever she opens her mouth these days, I wish I'd just let her drown out there, gone back up the lighthouse steps, and had a smoke instead."

He still thought he'd saved me all those years before. That somehow, the Queen of Atlantis had needed a lifeguard. Those good, kind, clean-cut All-American boys comforted him, hugged him (manfully), said they understood him. Nobody deserved a wife like me.

And so my husband put me away. In the gentler, medical wing of Davy Jones's Memorial. For my own protection, they said. So I could heal. So Megalodon couldn't find me. So they'd know I was safe. But really, so they'd feel better. So they could get back to the show already in progress. It was just so *messy*, the whole wife-and-kid thing. Doesn't go with the outfit. Leave that shit for a Very Special Episode and get back to prime time! I laughed in his face when he signed me over to the doctors.

"I'm sorry, John. I just didn't get it."

"What are you talking about, Bayou?"

"I thought we were a punkrage anthem for the ages. You and me against the world. But all you wanted was a groupie. You could get over Angus dying—*Azure* dying—you could stomach a psychotic shark out for your blood. But you couldn't share the fucking mic.

So, do what you do best, John. Smash everything around you and let someone else clean it up. Go be special in your shitpile world of nobodies and leave me locked up with the wreckage of us. Maybe someday you can tell a morning talk show about your crazy wife and watch the ratings soar. I'm not crazy; I just hate my life, you fuck."

John hasn't come to visitors' day in years. My cousin Baleen is running the joint out there. As far as my doctors are concerned, Queen Bayou is a quiet, easy patient. She doesn't cause any trouble. She floats in her room and doesn't bother anyone and every once in a while, she sings real soft to the waves: *Blue is the color of love, my darling. Everything good is blue*. As far as anyone can tell, my husband plans to leave me here forever, a gun on the mantle, a hammer under glass. *In Case of Emergency, Break Plot*.

But you know what? Megalodon was right. The sea is full of doors. And all the doors lead to power.

One of them leads here.

THE HELL HATH CLUB VS. THE JUNGIAN SUBCONSCIOUS

The evening crowd starts drifting in through the frosted-glass door of the Lethe Café, doing that familiar little Charleston of wriggling out of coats and hats and conversations about grandchildren, and started back home in the blackstone rows. They're dressed beautifully, pearls and half-Windsors all around. A woman swathed in a glittering red swirl of amazingness hands her matching red fur coat to Neil the gargoyle, who kisses her hand with his wolfy lips.

"I wish they'd've buried me in something like that," sighs Daisy Green, curled up next to me, shoes off, bare feet tucked under her in the long, curved booth. She lays her head on my shoulder. She smells like the best part of a nice city, the part that's all lights and laughter and tidy, blooming trees. "I never wore anything like this a day in my life."

Daisy Green is stuck for all eternity in a modest black sack dress with a ridiculous lace Peter Pan collar. An Amish schoolmarm would cringe and ask for something with a little more flair. Her gorgeous butter-blond hair is frozen in a straight homeschool braid, and her shoes were clearly fished out of a lost-and-found bin at the funeral home. She's Miss America dressed as Norman Bates's mother.

"You and me both," I sigh. I'm no better. I've got the dress I graduated in, and it's *plaid*.

HEAR ME, O YE MIGHTY LIVING!

Down here in Deadtown, all us boys and girls are cursed to wear whatever the hell you buried us until the heat death of the universe, so give us a goddamn break! The stars will burn out and the oceans will boil before I can take these stupid plastic butterfly barrettes out of my hair and wipe off the Carefree Coral lipstick some mortician thought looked *timeless*. Well, it's pretty fucking timeless now, and I hate it like hellfire. I've seen men in powder blue suits and long-toed loafers trying to claw them off in the alley. Girls bending scissors on their black wool twinsets. Daisy's braid might as well be made out of stone. But some people get lucky, like Miss Red over there, savoring her empty wineglass. Somebody thought to take care of her. Buried her in a prom dress or her favorite gown. Let her hair hang loose and full. Must be nice.

We order another round. Outside the Lethe's big, dark windows, the streetlights flicker. It's starting to rain.

"Turn on the radio, would you, Neil?" calls Miss Red. The bartender reaches up above the top shelf. With one thick, steel-colored claw, he turns the dial on a big deco monstrosity like flipping the tap on a pint of beer. Static glugs out and the Lethe Club goes quiet. Well, not *totally* quiet. The dead are a loud bunch. But while the moon never sets and the dark never fades in Deadtown, the clock on the wall says 5 PM and that means one thing in this neighborhood. A voice as warm and rich as the head on a chocolate stout pours down from the speaker.

"You're listening to DPR, Deadtown Public Radio, the Voice of the Underworld. That was Quarter Inch Bleed with their hit 'Cyan Eyes Make Cyanide.' And now, ghosts and gargoyles, dames and demons, boys and beasts, spirits dire and kindly, sit back and let your favorite rag-and-bones girl cart your cares away. It's time for

Daisy Chain, the talk of Deadtown, with your dear departed host, Daisy Green."

Daisy smiles against my shoulder. It's her voice. It's her show. She likes to listen to herself in a crowd. Seeing them listening. Seeing them care *so fucking much* about what she has to say. Being in two places at once is no problem in Deadtown. Her echo is down at the studio, wearing huge headphones and making love to a microphone, while she drinks with us. Down here, people remember her from the movies, but they only mention the really arty ones. Down here, her voice is always the best it ever was on some perfect day after a good night's sleep, no cigarettes in a week, and a quart of honey in her tea.

Down here, it's always her best show.

DAISY GREEN SAYS I LOVE YOU

Hello, Deadtown, my darling. You look wonderful tonight. Just as beautiful as the day we met.

I've been thinking a lot about rules lately. About karma, I guess, even though most people just *viciously* abuse that word. They don't give one spangly fuck about the wheel of becoming and unbecoming. They just want to rub themselves raw against the idea that bad things only happen to bad people. Samsara is just something they name their cat. But the longer I'm dead, the more I think the universe is a big blackboard with rules scrawled all over it in chalk and stardust and it's just that the damn thing is flipped over and turned away from us so we can't see anything but the eraser, which is death, hitting the floor. Write out your life one thousand times, kid, or you'll have to come back and finish tomorrow.

Deadtown, maybe it's time to spill my very specific and personal beans into your soup bowl. Maybe it's time to answer those questions you're all far too polite and gracious to ask.

Bad things happen to bad people. Bad things happen to good people. Bad things happen to okay people. Bad things happen to everyone. Good things happen to . . . well, somebody, probably. Somebody somewhere else.

But I think I've figured out one of the rules on the other side

of that great squeaky cosmological blackboard. It's not a big rule. No need to carve it in clay tablets with fiery finger paint and proclaim it from any kind of mount. It wouldn't even make the Macrocosm Top Ten. But it's there, I think. Crammed in at the bottom just under *Light Is Both a Particle and a Wave* but above *Don't Cut in Line*. Are you ready? Here it is: Daisy Green's Zero-Sum Law of Luck.

Luck is a finite and rare substance in the universe, like palladium or cobalt. To use it, you have to take it from somebody else.

I'm pretty sure Misha Malinov stole my luck.

He didn't mean to. They never *mean* to do anything in the beginning. But a superhero is like a black hole. They bend everything around them without even thinking about it. And they'd better be lucky as a goddamned leprechaun wearing a rabbit-foot coat on lottery day, or they'll never get through one single fight with a D-list villain. So, they just . . . suck it up from everyone around them. Trust me, kiss one hero and the coin will never land your way again for the rest of your life. And all that shit, all that horror they can leap in a single bound . . . all that shit has to land somewhere.

I had a little luck, for a little while. Not born-a-Kennedy or cash-out-your-stocks-in-1928 luck, but something small, something all my own I could fold up and keep at the bottom of my sock drawer. My dad moved us from Lewiston, Maine, to Brighton Beach when I was six, so I'd never have to save up enough on my own to move to New York. My mother was in a terrible car crash when I was a baby, but she lived, and she only has a little limp. You'd barely notice it. I was born looking the way most people secretly figure a Real American Girl™ should look—blond, blue-eyed, good figure, nice teeth. No major allergies or crippling anxieties. A good mind for math and a flair for performing. I've played Juliet more times than you want to know about. Directors look at me and think, *That's* just *the kind of girl you fall in love with the minute you see her at your parents' garbage party and kill yourself over a week later.* I drew good cards from a stacked deck, and I played them well.

Until I met Misha Malinov.

You know him as Mikey Miller, the Insomniac, the Coney Island Crusader, Working Class Warrior and Skee-Ball Champion of the World.

But when my dad buckled me in next to a shy, worried-looking ten-year-old boy on the Cyclone at Luna Park, his name was Misha Malinov, and he hadn't slept in six years. He only spoke a little English and he had these big brown eyes like the kind of liquor grandfathers drink and he was *way* luckier than me. You have to be, if you get yourself born in a place called Pripyat in 1982 and you think it'd be pretty sweet to see the '90s. His parents worked at the nuclear plant, right up until it decided to shit molten poison into the Ukrainian forest and make sure everyone would remember its name forever. They died trying to save the machinery. By the time his aunt and uncle brought him to America, Misha knew something was very wrong with him, even if he didn't know what. By the time we rode the Cyclone together, Miasma was already coming through to our world on a semi-regular schedule.

We didn't date in high school or anything. I recognized him at the start of sixth grade, Mikey-not-Misha-thank-you-miss, sitting in the front row, flinching if Mrs. Kendrick moved too quickly, drawing in his notebook in a way that looked like he was taking notes. But I had my own thing going back then, and that's how I kept my luck as long as I did. He saw me play Juliet for the first time, and

Mary Magdalene and Ophelia and Laura in *Glass Menagerie* and Emily from *Our Town*, High School Drama's Greatest Hits. He always came. He waited after curtain call to tell me I was wonderful. And that was it. Mikey-not-Misha got nervous around people, and the longer he had to be around someone, the more nervous he got, until he looked like he was going to shake apart right in front of you and you'd see that he'd just been a bunch of little kids in a trench coat all along. I know what you're thinking—*that* old story. Pretty, popular girl doesn't pay attention to the shy boy who loves her, film at eleven. But he didn't give anyone a chance to get close. He was trying to save us from day one.

If he talked to someone for too long, Miasma would come after them.

But I didn't know that then.

I went out to Hollywood; Mikey Miller went to law school. I got an Apple commercial and then a recurring role in the latest iteration of *Gorgeous White Teens Inventing Problems for Themselves*, a show that can never be canceled, only renamed. The lead actor took my glasses off in the Christmas episode and discovered I was beautiful. After we cut for the day, he locked me in his trailer and wouldn't let me out till I blew him. Whatever. It's not like I hadn't read a book about Hollywood in my life. Nothing unexpected. I flew home for the holidays, ate turkey and ham, went out for beers with the prodigal gang of returning collegiate conquerors. Beers turned into martinis, martinis turned into shots, I ended up back in Mikey Miller's dorm room in the city, fucking like it was the end of the world. When I came, I saw sunflowers opening in my mind, yellow and red as summer.

He wouldn't let me stay over. He looked so sorry and miserable as he pushed me out the door. It stung. It always stings when there's this whole story going on and you're really just a B-plot walk-on who only got a look at three pages of the script.

When I deplaned in LA, I'd been written off to make room for an exciting new accidental-murder storyline. My character had jetted off to Denmark as an exchange student. Fucking Denmark.

Was that how it started? One night with Misha Malinov and you lose your oldest dream. I thought I'd bounce back. I booked a dog food commercial. A spring catalog. Sang a jingle for a car insurance company. And that was it. LA went dry as Last Chance Gulch for me. After all, in California, every girl looks like me. We're a clone army of former Juliets with peroxide pistols on our hips. Money ran out, and I was honorably discharged from the ranks. I moved home to sort my shit out, and, well, Misha's new practice needed a secretary. I needed rent. I'm not too proud to file and make coffee. But it stung. Juliet doesn't answer phones for eight hours a day. Ophelia might. Laura, definitely.

We fell back into old patterns. Brooklyn and sunflowers. But he still never let me stay over.

When my friends back in California asked what I was up to, I said I'd moved to Denmark. *Hej! Jeg ville ønske at du var her!*

I stayed late at the office one night in December. It's funny; the case seemed so important then, and now I can't remember one single thing about it. Nobody v. No one. Briefs and affidavits and depositions, oh my! I didn't see him come in, but you never do. I just looked up from my cup of toxic waste–dump coffee and my sanity went down for a nap. This *thing* towered over me, just staring with those eyes like holes punched through to hell. Seven, eight feet tall, wearing a brown leather duster and a plague doctor's mask with glass gas-mask goggles bolted into it. The beak was so long it covered his chest, and there was nothing inside the mask, nothing. Just blackness and heat and the absolute certainty that nothing you could possibly do in this world had any meaning at all.

Miasma. In the flesh, as much as he ever is.

Miasma reached out for me—his hand was all bone. Then it was straw. Then it was my father's hand. Then Misha's. Then the electric lights of Luna Park and the Cyclone twisted into fingers, a palm, a fist . . . and I was falling into the lights, down into the midway and the wooden roller coaster slats and the game with those little plastic horses lurching ahead on the big green board, stopping, shuddering forward again. The plastic jockeys turned to leer at me; their faces came alive—my father, my mother, my agent, laughing and laughing, the handsome monster who took off my glasses for the world to see, Romeo, Hamlet, George from Grover's Corners, Tom Wingfield screaming about opium dens, and Mikey Miller, poor, kind Misha Malinov. One by one, they caught fire and the fire was sickly black. I screamed. I screamed like a girl in a movie. I'd always hated that scream. I thought, nobody *really* screams like that. But in the pinch, I was as good as any final girl drenched in corn-syrup blood.

The plastic jockey–Misha broke free of the pack and roared off the electric board, growing bigger and bigger as I screamed. He wasn't plastic anymore; he was real, and alive, and kicking the absolute *shit* out of the Halloween costume that had come to kill me. I never had any idea he could move like that. Maybe nobody *can* move like that. When Miasma and the Insomniac get down to business, you can't tell what's actually happening. Misha drove his fist through the thing's chest and dragged something out—not a heart but a wriggling, writhing mass of black-violet nightworms that hissed into smoke in his hand. The leather duster and the plague doctor's mask collapsed instantly. The lights of Luna Park went out in my head, the midway vanished, the slats of the Cyclone blew away, and we were standing in the office again. I dropped my coffee. Misha caught it.

And, loyal listeners, thus began the happiest days of my life.

Mikey Miller explained everything. Since that terrible day when Chernobyl bled out and his parents died, Mikhail Dmitrivich Malinov had not slept for one solitary second. And, it seemed, in losing this, he'd gotten everything else imaginable. He told me what he could do and it sounded like a little boy's Christmas list. *Dear Santa, I have been very good this year you can ask anybody they will tell you how good I am. I would like teleportation, super strength, the ability to travel through other people's dreams, heightened senses, and if my sweat could also make regular humans absolutely fucking trip balls, that would be awesome. Oh, and also peace on earth and goodwill toward men. Love, MM.*

"Can you look into my dreams?" I asked shyly. I expected him to say no, actually. Like, the power of love kept my secrets safe. But he nodded. Okay, then. I remembered the sunflowers opening in my mind. That sweat thing is a fucking curveball, even in the superpower lineup.

"Have you?"

His face did the oddest thing. It's like it was trying to look *ashamed* and *embarrassed* but fell over and landed smack in the middle of *kind of pretty proud*. And he nodded yes again. I went a little cold inside. I said:

"Don't. It's not fair. You've kept your secret from me for all these years. I get to keep some from now on."

In all that teleporting and hitchhiking into the dream-swamps of the greater boroughs, he'd brought something back with him. He couldn't remember when he'd first dreamed about the man in the plague-doctor mask. It might have been all the way back in Ukraine. In Pripyat. It came for him covered in radioactive slime and his mother's blood, staring through that medieval face and industrial eyes at a helpless child, whispering the same thing over and over: *You will never belong anywhere. Everywhere you go will die.*

Year by year, that thing got stronger, got bigger and more solid, could stay in the real world longer, and hated Misha Malinov more. Whenever Misha so much as looked at someone for too long, Miasma would begin to stalk them, invade their mind, tearing them apart to find out what had drawn Misha's attention. But lately the creature had gone freelance, walking the streets alone, feeding on human hope and longing and, well, not to put too fine a point on it, blood. Meat. Misha became a hero, not to fight some nebulous idea of "crime" but to fight the monster of his childhood nightmare. The Insomniac, hero of the wee hours.

"But it's okay now!" I said. "You killed him! I saw you pull out his nasty worm heart! It's over now, baby. It's done."

Misha sighed. The Insomniac walked over to the pile of leather still lying on the floor where Miasma had disintegrated. He picked up the long bone mask in one hand and walked past my desk, into his office. He waved me over to the supply closet with a big half-dead fern in front of it, and opened the door.

Inside, hundreds of plague-doctor masks hung on the walls in neat, identical rows.

"Miasma is a bad dream. You can wake up all you want. He comes back the next night just the same."

And that's the truth. Some of you out there probably know the score firsthand. The Insomniac hunted Miasma every night and every night he ripped out that thing's ultraviolet heart and every night the creature turned up again fresh as laundry.

But Misha was so happy after that. He didn't have to hide from everyone. He had somebody who knew him. Who could really see him. Who would clap her hands instead of freaking the fuck out when he shivered and wrinkled along the edges—like something you see out of the corner of your eye when you haven't slept for a week—and teleported across the office. And for a while, it was good. For a while, it was thrilling. For a while, I was part of something so fantastic and unusual and big and secret. I knew something no one else knew. I felt special. Like my superpower was loving him. For a while . . . for a while, it was like we were starring in simulcast TV shows. *By day, Mild-Mannered Mr. Miller toils nobly in the halls of the American Justice System with a little help from his Girl Friday! But the real work begins at night! The Insomniac guards his sleeping city, the paladin of Luna Park, keeping the world of dreams safe for all mankind.*

And then there was *The Daisy Show*. *By day, the adorable Daisy Green performs intellectually stultifying secretarial duties and watches her youth slough off her into a filthy coffeepot! But by night, she shreds her soul to pieces worrying and waiting for her big strong man to come home from a hard night's labor! Will he come back dead or not dead this week? Stay tuned!*

The only life in my life lay in the crossover episodes. *View their staunch moral fiber! Their witty banter! Their modestly separate beds!* When he came home. When he told me how it had all gone down out there. When he ate whatever bullshit I'd baked to pass the time and the fear like it was the only food he'd ever seen. When he lay next to me after all those sunflowers stopped blossoming in my head and told me how beautiful I'd looked on television. He watched all my episodes. He was so happy. I made him happy. But all the while, I was disappearing. Drinking from two cracked cups every night, one marked TERROR and one marked BOREDOM. I couldn't relax. I gave him every ounce of my will. *Just don't die. Just don't die.* I stopped sleeping too, but it didn't give me magic powers. You can't sleep when someone you love is maybe dying, maybe drowning in the East River, maybe bleeding out in the Meatpacking District, maybe vanished back into whatever helldream vomited Miasma out in the first place. He always came home right at the moment when I knew in my heart that this time, he was definitely dead.

I know you're listening, Paige. Hear me when I say it's not so nice, to be the girl waiting in the window. Most of the time, you just wanna chuck yourself out.

My hair started to fall out. I got a Xanax prescription I didn't tell him about. That worked for a while. I could laugh again. Flash a prescription-strength smile. Boy, I was living the Betty Friedan dream! A roast in every pot and anxiety pills in every stomach! I was disappearing into his life. I only came alive when he was around to look at me and pay attention to me and fill me in at the edges. That's the sad truth of poor, stupid Juliet's life. If she'd lived, she'd have gone to see that priest anyway, to float her out of the crush of wifehood on a sweet opiate sigh. And I wasn't even anybody's wife! Days went by when the only person I saw was Misha. I started to look forward to Miasma showing up and drop-kicking me into a hallucinogenic ball-pit of the mind. At least that was interesting.

How is life in Denmark, Daisy? Is it all mermaids and pastries and free health care?

Oh, ja. Wouldn't trade it for anything.

And then my parents died.

Plane crash. They got bumped off their flight to Paris for Dad's endocrinology conference but managed to snag a first-class upgrade on another airline. I imagine they rushed across JFK to make it, giggling like kids and toasting when they buckled in, thrilled with their good fortune. Then boom, splash, sunk to the bottom of the sea. And everything after that was just . . . bad dreams.

I left. I loved Misha, but I left. Canceled *The Daisy Show*, my Xanax prescription, and my broadband and lit the fuck out. Didn't have the cash to get back to California. Didn't have the cash for much of anything but a suitcase and a bus ticket south. Guignol City has a pretty hopping theater scene, but most importantly, it wasn't New York, it wasn't Brooklyn, and it wasn't Denmark.

Here we go. This is the story I know you want to hear. The one you've all been nice enough to never ask me about. My origin story.

When you're as lucky as Misha, when the monster under your bed never gets you once, when the girl you loved from afar loves you back, loves you enough to become set dressing in your big, splashy, high-budget drama, it has to come from somewhere. And Misha's luck came from everyone around him. He was a vampire of luck. His parents back in Ukraine, my parents toasting with airline champagne, his clients, his college roommate Jimmy Keeler who lost his scholarship, his girlfriend, his sobriety—and me.

I landed on my feet in California, working, hustling, doors opening, footlights shining. It was easy, like high school. But Guignol City laughs at the Juliet Army and puts out cigarettes on their tits. I couldn't get hired to twirl a sign outside a cell phone store, let alone legit acting work. I crashed on my friend Alexandra's couch—she played Nurse to my Juliet then and now. We went to clubs together at night, my Nurse and I, dressed up in our best neon and rain, the clubs where casting scouts were rumored to gather, hunting them like birdwatchers chasing reports of a rare emerald-crested plover, and with about as much luck. Men bought me drinks but no one wanted to buy me, except in the most obvious way.

But hey, Occam's razor, right? Sometimes, the most obvious solution is the best.

I remember my first time. He wasn't too bad-looking and he didn't pretend he was producing a gritty new police procedural or anything. Just lonely and frumpy and awkward and shy, which, in Guignol City, makes you a lamb already half-slaughtered. Said his name was Charlie. Told him mine was Delilah. Couldn't resist a little literary flair. He had a loft on Polichinelle Street with this huge skylight. I could see the moon and all the pink and purple and green lights of the seedy street signs rippling below like the aurora borealis. Charlie kissed me and kissed me and what do you know? I was on stage again. I was the prettiest girl this guy was ever gonna fuck. I'd star in his fantasies forever. By the lights of Guignol City, I gave the performance of a lifetime. All the great whores of the stage animated my body: Cleopatra, Salome, Sally Bowles, Mary Magdalene, Fantine, Helen of motherfucking Troy. I gave them all to Charlie, my audience of one, my biggest fan, at least for a few minutes. No sunflowers flared yellow or red in my brain, but Charlie's eyes became the cameras I'd been chasing all my life.

When he finished, I stretched up, kissed his eyelids, and whispered, *I love you*. My curtain call. My bow, before a red curtain, roses flying, applause shaking the chandeliers.

For a moment, it was even true. I loved all of them for a moment or two. Every man I ever fucked. I am a professional. I felt Ophelia's obsession and Laura's need and I felt the love I gave.

He whispered back, *My real name is Joe.*

It's a ridiculous superpower. The smallest of the small. But they always told me their real names.

That was the first and last time I let a customer fall asleep in my arms. He paid me a hundred bucks and boiled me a very sentimental egg for breakfast. I think if I'd wanted to, I could have stayed and Joe would have married me by Thursday. I never saw him again. I took my money down to the Malfi Diner on Pigalle Avenue and ordered myself a disgustingly huge, greasy Salisbury steak, waffles with strawberries and whipped cream, a tower of potato latkes and applesauce, a bucket of lamb vindaloo, and a peanut butter milkshake. I ate every bite. It tasted like a future. It tasted like life. I didn't feel ashamed. I didn't feel the urge to run to the nearest confessional and barf up my soul onto some poor unsuspecting padre. *The Daisy Show* was back on, in a new time slot, with an all-new cast. And after each and every Very Special Episode, I said, *I love you*. Even if he hit me or choked me a little too hard or called me his wife's name or called me a fucking cunt whore or broke three of my fingers for no fucking reason what the hell. *I love you. I love you*. A real actress never falters. She gives the audience what they came for. And love is all anyone comes for.

I stayed on with Alexandra, but now I paid half the rent and graduated from couch-crashing to bedroom-burrowing. We had an Alex and Daisy movie night every Tuesday, shine or rain. That was one of her phrases. Alex hated clichés, but she knew her whole life was one, really, so she settled for a little word-shuffling and dayed it a call. Misha phoned every week. I said I was fine. *Audition after audition, darling, you wouldn't believe it. No, no visits from You Know Who. I think he's lost interest in little old me.*

One night, I caught me an honest-to-god emerald-crested plover. A casting director. Arlecchino Films. Real name: Frank. He liked being scolded. He liked my hair. He liked the fading bruise on my ribs. When I finished punishing him, he told me to come down to the studio in the Medici Quarter and he'd pay me two grand to do my act on camera. Well, why not? Maybe my luck was coming back. Peeking out at me from behind this balding, freckled man who liked being called a disappointment while he jerked himself off. Who liked to watch. It's not like my parents could get mad.

And thus, Delilah Daredevil was born.

There you have it, Deadtown. The definitive answer. *Where have I seen that girl before? Where have I heard that dulcet voice?* You've seen me on my knees; you've heard me moan. You know me from movies. Just not the kind that wins Oscars.

Becoming a porn star is pretty much exactly like becoming a superhero. One day, an intrepid, fresh-faced young woman discovers that she has a talent. She chooses a new name—something over the top, flamboyant, a little arrogant, with a tinge of the epic. Somebody makes her a costume—skintight, revealing, a flattering color, nothing much left to the imagination. She explores her power, learns a specialty move or two, sweats her way through a training montage, throwing out punny quips here, there, and everywhere. She inhabits an archetype. She takes every blow that comes her way like she doesn't even feel it. Then she goes out into the big bad night and saves people from loneliness. From the assorted villainies that plague the common man. From despair and bad dreams. From tedium. Oh, sure, her victories are short-lived. She finishes off her foes in one glorious masterstroke, but the minute she's gone, all the wickedness and darkness of the scheming, teeming world comes rushing back in. But when you need her, here she comes to save the day, doing it for Truth, Justice, and the American Way.

At least, that's how it felt at first.

I felt like I understood Misha, finally, in a way I never could before. I liked to think I could have called him up and exchanged stories with him. Tips, techniques. Finally, we both had a secret identity. A By Day and a By Night. Sometimes, I even dialed a digit or two of his phone number before deciding that a good Russian Orthodox boy probably wouldn't see the wonderful symmetry in our story. I even wore a mask! It was my signature. A little dark red domino mask with red rhinestones at the corners of my eyes and long ribbons that rippled over my breasts or down my back like blood. Very commedia dell'arte! Everything old is new again and everything new is a fetish. I was finally where I wanted to be—at the center of attention, watched by thousands of adoring eyes, the camera firmly on me. My costars were cheerful, uncomplaining, and interchangeable. Boy Fridays waiting for me to come. Repeatable Romeos, too like the lightning, which doth cease to be 'ere one can say it lightens. And in the beginning, everyone treated me like Elizabeth goddamned Taylor.

I "lost" my "virginity" in *The Opening of Delilah Daredevil*, seduced the President in *Delilah Deep*, wore a toga for at least the first five minutes of *Delilah Daredevil vs. Nero's Fiddle*, brought Satan to his knees in *The Devil in Miss Dare*, went up against the spirit world in *Ghostlusters*, got to find out what it's like to kiss (a lot of) girls in *Delilah Daredevil vs. the Amazon Women of Planet* XXX, even got to wear wings and a corset in A *Midsummer Night's Delilah* and say one full line of actual Shakespeare. Okay, it was: *Masters, spread yourselves*. But still. It was a world of yes. All my movies got sequels; all my lights were green. *Delilah Daredevil Does Detroit, Delilah Daredevil Does Damascus, Delilah Daredevil Does the Danube*, and, eventually, inevitably, *Delilah Daredevil Does Denmark*.

But becoming a porn star is pretty much *exactly* like becoming a superhero. You start strong, bursting out of nowhere, a bird, a plane, your name on a million needy lips, your name in the papers, your name up in lights, your greatest hits on constant repeat. You're *the* fantasy—someone so strong and beautiful nothing can hurt them, not even the worst shit anyone can imagine. In the first flush of it all, you're so convinced of the rightness of your mission statement that you practically glow when the bad guy's final spasm stains your mask. The camera loves you. It just *feels good* to throw down. You do it for fun, just to feel your own strength. When you're new, everyone's so fucking impressed with your skill and style. All these roaring, power-drunk men line up just to go one round with you. You blow them all down like paper dolls to rave reviews and the key to the red-light district. But time passes and it hurts more than you let on. You bandage yourself after hours, alone, in a phone booth with filthy windows, wrapping your wounds tight so you can keep fighting the good fight day after day. You get tired now. You get jaded. You get older. And after a while, they begin to despise you. It's not *interesting* for you to come out on top every time. To watch your Saturday night marquee smile pop-flash at the end of every climactic scene. You need to keep up your numbers. You need to keep those eyeballs *transfixed*, Miss Thing. It's not enough to just work on your craft. You gotta keep up with the times, appeal to modern sensibilities. You have to do something more extreme. Darker. Grittier. More real. You need to be cut down a little. Let 'em see you vulnerable. Let 'em see you bleed.

So, no more cheerful SuperWhore, Guignol City's Girl with a Heart of Gold and a twinkle in her eye. That's last year's hotness and it's this year's time to burn. The Delilah Daredevil name doesn't move copies anymore. But Daisy Green still needs to pay her landlord, and once the world's seen what you can do, you can't squeeze your way back into the normal world. People recognize you. They avert their eyes. They whisper, *Didn't our barista save Manhattan? Didn't she battle the Amazon Women of Planet XXX? Didn't she take three guys at once with a riding bit in her mouth?* Yes, she did, cats and kittens. And she wasn't ashamed of any tiny bit of it until they decided it would be hot to make her ashamed.

Misha stopped calling every week. Every fortnight, then every month. I told myself it wasn't because he'd seen my recent work. Though I'd certainly seen his. He'd joined some superpower frat called the Union. They destroyed an underwater lair and got to speak at the UN. Misha gave the commencement address at Harvard. My whole life was just a little rummaging backstage while sets changed for his. So much wonder in his world, siphoned from the gas tanks of we bitter few, dying by inches so he can do the impossible, over and over again. Luck is a zero-sum game. There's only so much to go around. Sometimes, I read his victorious headlines and thought, *Was that a part I didn't get? My parents having a wonderful time in Paris and bringing me back a crappy miniature Eiffel Tower? Delilah Daredevil Does Legitimate Theatre? What dribbled out of me that blossomed into glory for him? Or did I just fuck it up myself?*

I turned on the Xanax fire hose again. That worked for a while. I could laugh. Flash my prescription smile. But come on, you know how this story goes. It's the same word. It's always been the same word. One hiding inside the other. I am a heroine, after all.

The first time was with Alexandra. Alex and Daisy's Tuesday movie night. We'd rented the action-packed black-and-white *Wuthering Heights* because we are who we are and Alex and me were never anything but high school girls blacked out on daydreams, misreading psychosis for love. As the child of many earnest federal drug education programs, I thought the first time I shot up would be dramatic. Ominous music, swooning, air thick with tension, *will she or won't she*? Surely, the world closes in on a girl making this momentous decision, the spotlight comes on for a real Hamlet-esque soliloquy on the nature of oblivion and the self-destructive impulses of man.

I popped a Xanax. Alex asked if I wanted something stronger. Cathy Earnshaw perished beautifully on our rabbit-eared TV. She tied me off and whispered, *Prince sweet, night good*. She slid the needle in like Sleeping Beauty's spindle, and for the first time in a year, sunflowers opened up in my mind, yellow and red as summer.

The rest is silence. Silence, and then a cough I couldn't shake, and then red marks on my skin like angry kisses, like spotlights, like the actual, terrible, unfor-fucking-givable cliché that I was. *The Daisy Show* was such a hack-fest. A product of its times. Heavy-handed, preachy, full of bullshit moralizing, and fucking *Christ* what a predictable finale! What is this after-school-special horse-shit? It's the kind of thing some asshole in Ohio gets a National Book Award for writing while he screws his grad students and cries his way to tenure. My boyfriend took all the magic and left me with nothing but the dregs of realism. *The Misha Malinov Show* was always the prime-time attraction. I'm just . . . some public-access embarrassment. I died in a free clinic in the left armpit of Guignol City and you know exactly what killed me so just nod piously and spare me the humiliation of stitching on my scarlet A. Someone who didn't know me at all grabbed a dress at Goodwill and put me in the ground at the public's expense. Finally, government funding for the arts!

The worst part of dying is that you never get to find out the end of the story. Did the Insomniac finally defeat Miasma? Fucked if I know. I didn't get that script. I was just a deep dark past, the battery of sadness hidden in the hero's heart. I was *Rosaline*, for fuck's sake. Juliet will show up in scene two and teach the torches to burn bright or whatever and I'd hate her, but let's be real, ladies and gentlemen, he'll suck her dry too, and we'll all meet her for tea down here at the Lethe Café. The play is still going. It's booked every night until the sun goes out. I'm just the local theater ghost.

And that's that, my darlings. The two hours' traffick upon our stage, complete with fatal loins! Not bad, really. Maybe I'll make it into a one-woman show. And you know, I am *glad* that we know each other now, *really* know each other, companion bosoms, from the heart of my bottom. *Delilah Daredevil Does Deadtown*. I love you. My dear departed, I love you so.

I'll take the first caller on line one.

THE HELL HATH CLUB VS. THE GIRL IN THE REFRIGERATOR

The moon strikes the dinner hour and the Lethe Café house band shuffles in, jangling and shattering the shinbone bell over the door. No loss—it'll grow back in the morning.

The whole time I was alive, I never loved a rock star like I love these four onyx-winged gargoyles with Christmas lights wrapped around their horns and pen-nib piercings running up and down their brimstone ears. Quarter Inch Bleed. Deadtown's putrefying punk sensation.

I'm so excited that somewhere up above me, somewhere up in the dirt, the heart I used to have gives one last thrilling, dusty thump.

We don't have much use for money down here except as interior decor. I've got a beaded curtain that's all old-as-fuck Greek drachmas. You know, the kind they used to put on corpses' eyes so they could cross the Styx. But the Styx isn't a river anymore. The underworld's come a long way since Helen and Medea and Iphigenia and Clytemnestra painted the town black—the original Hell Hath Club. Deadtown's like a dear old grandfather trying to use the Internet. Slow as snails on quaaludes, but he does his best to get with the times. You can find the Styx in the pipes nowadays. Deadtown Municipal Waterworks. We drink it out of our faucets, we bathe in it, it shoots out of fire hydrants on warm nights and all the neighborhood children come out to jump and dance in the spray. And all those coins come spurting up out of the drains, float down the gutters, fire like bullets out of the hydrants into the sky. So, we do have money, but money isn't *currency*. It doesn't matter. Not here.

What matters is *entertainment*. Eternity takes *forever*. The infinite expanse of time just does not know when to quit. The dead fear boredom the way mortals fear death. And it's not like you can kill yourself to escape. Deadtown will do anything for the delight of distraction. When you don't need anything anymore, the only thing you need is stories, and songs, and beauty, and spectacle. That's the good stuff. The stuff that reminds us who we are. Remember that bit in *The Odyssey* where Odysseus (my upstairs neighbor and a *total* dick, by the way) brings the dead back to life for about half a second by feeding them blood? No. That's disgusting. He brought them back to life by telling them his *story*. The blood was his own weird fetish. The dead don't turn out for gore; they come for the show.

We get them all when they die, all the nightclubs that ever shut, every theater that burned to the ground, every museum that lost funding and got remodeled into condominiums, every amusement park sold for scrap or left to be slowly claimed by weeds and sun. Just like our triceratops pies and great auk eggs over easy. The minute a TV show gets canceled, a book goes out of print, a play closes, some soldier blows up a statue, a dance goes out of style, a song gets forgotten, that's the minute we get them. (I swear to god, we are *never* going to get Harry Potter and I am *not* okay about it.) The Alexandrian Library has a line around it like Studio 54, you wouldn't believe it—and Studio 54's waiting list goes all the way back to the Paleolithic era. The gang's all here, the artists too, writers, musicians, painters, actors. I know you don't *want* to die and it probably keeps you awake some nights, the idea of everything that is you ceasing to be and all your works turning to dust, but down here you can see most of the Beatles playing the Hanging Gardens of Babylon. Oscar Wilde sings Paul's parts, Sappho hits the drums, Sojourner Truth and Basquiat do spoken word while Joan of Arc and Judy Garland perform an interpretive dance, and Laurence Olivier reads the phonebook during the set break. It's not all bad.

But Quarter Inch Bleed is homegrown. Local gargoyles made good. When they play, I feel like they're playing my life. Everyone feels that way. They're kind of . . . post-punk post-pop hipster rock sludgemetal folk-industrial techno-blues alt-grunge cabaret torch singers. You know, soul music. They start setting up on the little Lethe stage, playing my secret favorite song: the rustling of sheet music and set lists, the coughing and quiet warm-up, the tuning of instruments, the squeak of speakers and amps, the last drags on cigarettes and popping of knuckles. The four of them arch their long black wings, run through a couple of tongue twisters to loosen up their muzzles, pluck a few strings, tap a few keys with their claws. They're all there, Stan and Jack and Alan and Gail, their brilliant fur shining in the moonlight, their horns glittering with festive electric lights.

The Hell Hath Club holds down a booth like a fortress. No one can budge us from our prime seats. The Lethe Café is crowded now, with more pushing in all the time. Daisy snuggles in closer to me. Pauline rolls her eyes and fishes a cigar out of her cleavage. Under the table, she and Bayou are holding hands. Julia flickers in and out in time to the noise and bustle of the café.

And then we hear it. A soft, awful sound sawing back and

forth under the honkings of Jack running through a D scale on his accordion. It's coming from behind the bar, behind the swinging kitchen doors. Crying. Wheezing. Teeth chattering. Neil's horned head snaps up, his canine ears twitching. His boiling red eyes fill with concern. But it's not his business, it's ours. We know that sound. The Hell Hath Club abandons their front-row-center seats without a word. The bartender holds the doors open for us with an onyx-scaled hand. We listen in the kitchen, surrounded by knives.

It's coming from the refrigerator.

Bayou heaves the door open with her muscled Atlantean arms. The frosted air clears. A woman sits on the floor of the industrial fridge, naked, her dark skin blue and white, her hair frozen, ice clotted around her shoulders, her thighs, her neck. Two huge bruises shaped like hands blacken her throat.

"*Fuck*," Polly breathes. Even she feels bad for the popsicle. "She's brand-new. How long you been dead, kitten?"

"Hello, broccoli," the girl whispers. "Hello, grape juice." She coughs. "Not from concentrate."

Death really knocks you sideways. When I died, I woke up in a pile of garbage under the Phlegethon Bridge. It's the roughest Monday morning you'll ever pull. I crouch down next to the woman. Tug her long, tightly curled, slowly melting hair away from her face. The ends shine bright blue. She keeps shaking and shivering, but the sobbing slows down.

"I'm Paige Embry," I say gently. "Whatever happened to you, you're perfectly safe now. What's your name?"

She looks up at me with wild golden eyes, her lip trembling, her eyelashes clumped together with frost like white mascara.

"Samantha," she croaks.

HAPPY BIRTHDAY, SAMANTHA DANE

Hello, broccoli.

Hello, grape juice, not from concentrate.

Hello, farm-fresh butter.

Hello, nonfat milk.

Hello, individually wrapped cheese slices that I hate but Jason won't stop buying. Hello, eggs from Nina's chickens. Hello, boysenberry yogurt I should have thrown out weeks ago. Hello, bell peppers I was going to use to make sesame beef stir-fry tonight. Hello, half-defrosted beef. Hello, peaches and rhubarb I bought to bake a pie I'll never bake now.

I wonder if Jason will shudder whenever he sees peaches once he finds me like this. Maybe he'll stop buying that crappy cheese. I wonder if he'll ever find me. If he comes soon, maybe I'll still make it. In the meantime, it's just you and me, extra chunky peanut butter. Just you and me.

There's something about getting strangled by a minotaur and stuffed into a refrigerator that really makes you consider your choices in life. I was gonna be famous, you know. Diane Arbus, Julia Margaret Cameron, Annie Leibovitz, fucking Ansel Adams, they'd have had nothing on Samantha Dane. That's what I chose. I chose art. I chose work. I chose a viewfinder and a darkroom and a

shutter speed like a butterfly's blink. And I chose Jason Remarque. If you snip one of those choices out, would I be spending this quiet Thursday night making sesame beef and watching cartoons instead of feeling my heartbeat slowly give up with a half-eaten rotisserie chicken scraping against my back? Life is just full of funny questions, isn't it?

Let's try this one: what if I'd found that stupid button instead of Jason?

He always told me he got it at an estate sale, though I have no idea what kind of estate sale would sell a shitty, ugly button clearly made with a home machine by some furious yet crafty '80s stonerpunk. It had a hand-drawn zombified bald eagle front and center with the words *The Wages of Sin Are Reaganomics* carefully inked in a circle around the poor thing's rotting wings. Our witty artist had turned his A's into anarchist symbols, obviously. The level of artistic ability on display topped out at "obsessively doodled in the Health Sciences textbook of a tenth-grader with borderline personality disorder." Jason saw it in a box of similar homespun antiestablishment arts and crafts items and bought it instantly. He pinned it on the I'm-an-edgy-artist-but-don't-make-a-thing-about-it-*man* leather jacket I bought him for Christmas and showed up to my birthday dinner proud as a peacock with a 4.0. *Hey, don't look at me like that, Sam. It spoke to me! I like an outraged political statement that's thirty years out of date. If they'd had one that said* Warren G. Harding Is the Anti-Christ, *I'd have grabbed that one, too. Occupy Yesterday, baby!*

It cost him $1.50.

It made him a god.

Not, like, Zeus or Shiva or anything. Not *God* god. One of the minor ones, the redneck backwoods cousins of the fancy cosmic pantheon that only people who actually speak ancient Greek have ever heard of. I'm not being catty about it, I promise. Even Jason would admit the rest of the Avant Garde have way better powers. But Jason's was the prettiest. No contest.

We met in art school in New York like we'd been cast in some kind of indie romance flick. I called him my manic pixie fucktoy. He silkscreened it onto a T-shirt and wore it to his thesis defense. I was photography, Jason was graphic design and emergent urban media, which is how tenure-tracks spell *graffiti* on your diploma. We were two peas in a student housing unit: young, on scholarship, profoundly convinced of our own genius, highly enamored of Adderall, fashionably cynical, and comically well-read. We had matching his-and-hers eating disorders. We both hated our parents. (His: hardware store owners. Mine: professional alcoholics.) We both dyed our hair with the same cheap beauty supply store goo: *#143 Lady Sings the Blues.* We were hateably adorable. Only art divided us: my work was all about permanence, capturing time and feeling and freezing it forever. His was devoted to ephemerality: temporary, illicit, testament to the vitality of the fleeting and the impossibility of the very permanence I worshipped.

I was always pretty good at writing those little cards that hang next to your pieces in galleries. All about the active verbs, man.

Jason started doing his thing long before graduation. We'd light out from the dorms after midnight, his backpack clanking and jingling with cans of paint, my camera strap snug around my neck—as if it ever left. He'd cover the side of a bank in a Warhol-style portrait of the guy on the cover of the Monopoly game's big round face, or spray a little medieval goblin on the door of every apartment block on the East Side that had voted majority Republican, or paint a graveyard on the parking lot of an NYPD station with the names of every person shot by police in the last year lovingly stenciled on the asphalt. Signed them all with a flamboyant drop-shadowed letter C. That was his *nom de paint*: Chiaroscuro.

See? Hateably adorable.

That kind of thing was hot shit back then. Street art, ninja galleries. Art wants to be free. The gallery system is a noose around the neck of the artist. You know. Jason didn't always go political; he re-created the unicorn tapestries on the walls of a public elementary school. He thought the kids would like it. Everyone likes horses. I shot him working. I shot people's faces when they saw him painting at 3 AM. I shot the finished pieces. I think the longest one of Jason's pieces lasted was seventy-two hours. They broke out the big rollers and painted over his goblins and gravestones real quick. Except for the unicorns. The school kept them. The kids changed the foursquare rules to require hitting every unicorn hunter in the face before you can win. Everyone likes horses.

Jason railed against the contemporary scene, the cults of personality, the eagerness with which other students talked about selling installation pieces to cancer hospitals or tech campuses. Me, I never minded the gallery system. It's a tight collar at worst, really. The summer after we graduated, I showed a series of my Chiaroscuro photographs at the Eugenia Falk Memorial Gallery. Everyone ate white cheese and white wine and said white things about my work. I called the series *The Gallery System Is a Noose Around the Neck of the Artist*. Sold like candy at fat camp.

When he bought that button, we'd just moved into the kind of apartment stand-up comics build sets around. How small *was* it? So far uptown, you're basically in Canada, am I right? But it was ours. We only had one roommate: our tech. When a photographer and a graphic designer love each other very much, their gear merges into one big lump of wires and monitors and reference books and laser cutters, then starts multiplying. But as a roommate, gear is kind. Pirated copies of Photoshop could not tell us to fuck quieter or stop having five-minute dance parties every hour on the hour. We spent a weekend turning the bathroom into my darkroom, packing the medicine cabinet with developing chemicals instead of shampoo.

"Art doesn't need to pee!" Jason crowed, and kissed me like he majored in it.

I stopped off at the pound on the way home from a grant-writing seminar and got a cat in lieu of an endowment. A big, fat Abyssinian, tragically born without whiskers. We named him MacArthur the Genius Cat and let him eat people food. It was a lifelike photographs capturing the early 2000s zeitgeist that people will be sick of seeing in special exhibitions a hundred years from now. If I'd been any happier, I'd have been a Prozac prescription.

Then a fucking hideous undead bird landed on our little world, shitting everywhere and squawking *The Wages of Sin Are Reaganomics* in the general direction of the next millennium.

I never told Jason this. I guess I probably never will. But that first time it happened was the most beautiful thing I ever saw. So beautiful I forgot to go for my camera, and I was *born* reaching for a camera.

At 2 AM, Wall Street is a ghost town. Almost countryside quiet, sodium streetlights throwing post-apocalyptic orange flames all over the empty roads, signs flashing HALAL and ATM and NEW YORK STATE LOTTO with no one to see them. Jason climbed a ladder wedged in an alley between two office buildings while I kept watch. I smiled at the comforting *whoosh-whoosh* sound of his spray can hitting a stencil of Alan Greenspan dancing with the Statue of Liberty while lasciviously grabbing her ass. The love of my life finished up the prongs on Liberty's crown, blew on the wet, bloodred paint, waited, and slowly peeled back the stencil. The moon squinted down skeptically. A little trite by her standards. Jason Remarque reached out his hand to scrape off a stray smudge above the Fed's giant doofy glasses.

Alan Greenspan and Lady Liberty stepped off the wall of the New York Stock Exchange and into the open air. The wind off the river seemed to inflate them like red balloons, their aerosolized paint-bodies puffing out of 2-D and into an impossible 3. The Chairman of the Federal Reserve took his hand off Liberty's ass and placed it gracefully around her waist, sweeping her into a silent, perfect Viennese waltz a hundred feet into the skyline and climbing. The Statue of Liberty reached forward and adjusted her dancing partner's glasses. The stray smudge of paint still floated above the frames where Jason had left it. We watched them, dumbfounded, unable to reconcile what we saw with, you know, *any possible goddamned definition of reality*. We thought we lived in a universe where gravity is a thing, time moves at one second per second, the gallery system is a noose around the neck of the artist, and movies aren't real life. Because that's all your brain can say for itself when something that can't happen happens in front of you: *It looks like a movie. Oh! We're in a movie now. That's okay, then. Movies can't hurt you. Oooh, look at that! Her torch just came on!*

We watched Alan Greenspan and the Statue of Liberty for about an hour. They got tired of dancing after about twenty minutes and flew up to the roof of the Stock Exchange, where they dangled their fuzzy red legs over the edge and swung them like kids on a swing set. They talked, but no sound came out. At one point, they really got stuck into something. Lady Liberty flipped him off and hopped down to hang out with Integrity Protecting the

Works of Man, but, as the figures decorating the Stock Exchange remained marble and not paint, they weren't much company for her. Finally, Alan and Liberty started to fade and disperse, coming gently apart into thousands of tiny flecks of the paint I'd picked up for Jason at Art Mart on my lunch hour.

It took us a while to recover enough to talk about what the fuck just happened. Blah, blah, blah: *did you see that/I can't believe it/it's impossible/did we get pranked/did we do all of the drugs and just forget that we did all of the drugs?* All the while, my brain cheerfully munched popcorn and babbled away: *I told you, we're in a movie now. See, we even sound like movie people sound. We're saying what movie people say. Everything is A-OK! Silly Samantha, the effects weren't even that great.*

"I made that happen," Jason whispered. MacArthur the Genius Cat kneaded his lap plaintively. *Make petting happen, please.* "Somehow. Do you think I can do it again?"

We didn't dare try it outside. The sun cannonballed obnoxiously through our windows. If it worked, everyone would see. He grabbed the smallest stencil from his "new" pile: a Roman-style double-headed imperial eagle in a Carolina Fried Chicken combo meal box with a side of fries. The fries had triggers and safeties and barrels: deep-fried assault weapons. Jason shook an Art Mart can of *Yellow #455A Last Week's Lemoncake* and emerged urban media onto a patch of wall behind our refrigerator.

This refrigerator. Oh. I guess that's what the New School kids call foreshadowing. Wow, it's *fucking* easy to miss in real life!

Spray, blow, wait, peel. Nothing.

"You held out your hand toward it. To get the smudgy bit," I reminded him.

"Oh, right! God, that feels lame."

Jason held out his hand. He waggled his fingers like a bad stage magician in an effort to feel less stupid doing this stupid thing.

Slowly, the double-headed imperial eagle sloughed off the wall, still stuck in its Carolina Fried Chicken combo box. It plopped onto the dirty floor behind the refrigerator (this refrigerator), dragging the box behind it like a two-legged rescue dog dragging its little puppy wheelchair through the park. The imperial bird-monster looked up at us and squeaked soundlessly. A couple of gun-fries fell out of their bag as that weird tiny yellow latex mutant squeezed past us into the kitchen, firing useless puffs of anti–military industrial complex paint into the dust bunnies. MacArthur lost his fucking *mind*. He shrieked—apparently, cats can shriek—and reared up on his haunches. Our little guy thundered toward the combo box of (really, let's be honest) muddled political messages. His paws scrabbled on the linoleum, flying out from under him with the excitement of the hunt, and thus, the Chris Farley of Abyssinians both pounced *and* fell on top of his prey. With a howl of triumph, MacArthur the Genius Cat chowed down on the symbol of the twelve-secret-herbs-and-spices might of Rome and Byzantium, ripping it in two and gobbling both halves up before we could yell *no, no bad kitty don't eat daddy's magic paint golem thingy!* We just stared at the Carolina Fried Carnage.

We figured out it was the button's fault very scientifically. I said, "It's that goddamned hipster anarchist shitbird," and Jason agreed. "What is with you and eagles right now?"

The only other new thing in our life was MacArthur, and when we asked whether he gave Jason superpowers, he just showed us his very self-satisfied butthole and waddled off in search of fallen gun-fries. No man left behind. Plus, it didn't work if Jason took the button off, and it didn't work for me if I put the button on. We promptly got very drunk and giggly and busy making vaguely leftist spray-paint animated action figures, which went on for a week or so before the Avant Garde showed up to play Officer Exposition and drink the last of our beer.

Not the whole Avant Garde. They don't all live in this dimension. See, the universe is kind of like a shitty apartment building. All the dimensions nice and separate and doing their own dimensional thing, only the walls are thin and the insulation is garbage and the roof leaks, so sometimes you can hear everyone else screwing and practicing bass and yelling about who forgot to take out the trash. Some people have the super's key ring and can just go rummage around in other people's stuff whenever they want. Some people are shut-ins.

Look at me analogizing like it's normal to know this stuff!

Anyway, Still Life and Greyscale came to lock us down, knocking at the door like FBI agents when they were all of six months older than us, considerably less employed, super invested in playing twin minotaur mages on an MMO called *Warlock and Key: The Online Adventure*, and called Simon and Nina.

Simon clapped his hands and said, "Let's all have a drink. We'll all need a drink."

I didn't move to get drinks. Because A, I'm not your waitress, guy; B, don't invite yourself into my booze, thanks; and C, Simon was in black and white. Like an old photo. Just sucked dry of color. Other than that, he looked like a normal twentysomething, a little sweaty, a little too big for the weddings-and-funerals suit he'd obviously felt the occasion deserved, but normal. Just desaturated. Greyscale. Nina looked like the human version of one of those insta-vintage photo filters. She dressed like she'd walked off the set of a 1970s kids' show: rainbow-striped shirt, suspenders, pink jeans, green-rimmed glasses, puffy black braids. Like she was gonna teach me about phonics in a minute.

I like Nina now. She keeps chickens because she likes them better than people, and for whatever reason, her powers don't work on chickens. My hands are tied behind my back but I can feel the brown eggs she dropped off last week resting in their carton. I asked her once:

"How come you play that computer game all the time if you have superpowers in real life? Isn't it boring? I wouldn't touch a game about filling out grant applications and freelancing for the AP, you know?"

Nina Batista petted my cat and whispered, "In the game, if I lose, nothing bad happens."

The situation was this: there were, in fact, such things as dimensions and cosmic battles and what amounts to magic even if it isn't *technically* magic. Superpowers existed. Superheroes existed. Supervillains *definitely* existed. Some of these powers didn't come from a person but from objects that sort of *chose* a person. The Avant Garde was a group of people who had these objects, and now Jason had one too. Nina Batista and Simon Stewart were Still Life and Greyscale. Jason would meet the Pointillist, Bauhaus, Turpentine, and Zeitgeist in due time.

"It's not really a button," Nina explained shyly, nodding toward the zombie eagle on Jason's coat. "It just looks like one in this reality. It's . . . a semi-sentient energy nexus embodying the power of one of the Seven Eidolons of Artifice, who live in the Imago Dimension. Godlike beings of pure emotion that feed on the vibrations created by all human art. We are their avatars. We fight for freedom and goodness on this plane of existence. Does that make any sense at all?"

Jason and I looked at each other and shrugged. "Sure," we said at the same time. "We grew up watching *Star Trek,* so . . ."

"Yeah, that doesn't even sound that weird," Jason finished for me.

Apparently, Jason's button was the sigil of the Chaotic White Eidolon. Simon won the Voracious Red Eidolon's cuff links in a Big Claw machine when he was twelve, and Nina stole a bracelet from a bodega in eleventh grade that turned out to belong to the Pacific Violet Eidolon. Whoops. Jason explained about the neo-imperial combo box and Alan Greenspan and the alien tentacle lizard CEO and the Civil War soldier with a smartphone and all the rest of our one-hour photos.

"What . . . what can you guys do?" he ventured.

"Shapeshift," said Simon.

"Freeze time," said Nina.

"Cool," said Jason.

A classic awkward silence descended. I snapped a picture. Couldn't help it. It's stuck on the outside of this refrigerator with a MOMA magnet.

Simon pinched his cuff links and pixelated into a black-and-white tabby cat. He trotted over to MacArthur, hoping the cat would be easier to talk to than humans. MacArthur smacked him in the face with one meaty paw and yawned.

Look, I had to spend a lot of Takeout Tuesdays with the Avant Garde. The truth is, Simon and Nina are the only ones who have anything in common besides having picked up a piece of inter-dimensional anti-fashion at some point in their lives and ended up with a really specific, terrifying, world-shredding new hobby. The Pointillist and Bauhaus couldn't even stand to look at each other. Meetings were like trying to make conversation at a middle-school dance.

It turned out Jason and I were entering a program already in progress. At least, Jason was. I guess I was just . . . the loyal viewership. There must be something in the water in New York. All the villain wannabes disembark at Port Authority and try to make it big. Just like everyone else. If you can destroy the world here, you can destroy it anywhere. Remember when the Arachnochancellor crowned himself Emperor of Chicago, time-shifted Lakeshore Drive into the colonial era, and mind-controlled pretty much the entire Midwest for the duration of the holiday shopping season? After Avast and the Unstoppable Id hit him in the head with Navy Pier, he gave that interview to the BBC from Sarkomand Sanatorium. He sat there whining into his iridescent exo-suit, *Yeah, but I didn't destroy* New York. *So, it barely even counts*.

So, Jason Remarque became the seventh member of the Avant Garde, and out they went to play Whac-A-Mole with the city's criminal element. The Pointillist was their big gun—he could reduce anything to its constituent atoms just by touching a truly hilarious pentagram choker straight out of a preteen goth's regular rotation. With the cosmic power of his Class of 1977 UCLA ring missing its oversize sapphire, Zeitgeist could command people like puppets. Bauhaus could click a tongue piercing with pop-art yellow frowny faces on either end and summon a gang of huge geometric dark-matter blocks that defended her (and only her, unfortunately) like she was their own best baby. And Turpentine could take you right out of the timeline if she dragged on an e-cigarette with a glowing blue tip. Like you'd never been born. At first, Jason didn't know how he could contribute. They seemed to have the bases covered. But soon enough, he was spraying up paint armies of presidents in clown suits, GMO zombie vegetables, mecha Disney princesses, and dinosaurs with gasoline nozzles instead of tiny, tiny arms.

You'd think with a roster like that, the Avant Garde would be unstoppable. But a lot of the Imago objects had changed hands lately, and almost everyone still had kinks to work out. Basically, every night turned into a live-action role-play of those endless Who Would Win in a Fight? arguments. They started small, the super-villain equivalent of back-alley muggers, small-timers who didn't even have brand names or grand plans yet. And because none of them felt so hot about killing, they held back. Jason came home hungry and bloody and conflicted. And high as Lady Liberty on his own supply of adrenaline.

I kept on part-time at Art Mart, freelancing the occasional shot of a press conference or a Knicks game, writing other students' theses. Before I knew it, I was our only income. Jason couldn't work; he slept most of the day and ran with the Garde at night. I hadn't taken a *real* picture in months. Just still lifes with current events and portraits of graduating seniors in pearl earrings. The darkroom slid back into being a bathroom again. I let my hair grow out—no more cash for relaxer or *Lady Sings the Blues*. MacArthur glared at me resentfully as he ate his dry food, remembering the halcyon days of Beef Bounty Feline Feast in a can. I was just lonely enough to create my own mage on *Warlock and Key*—a wombat necromancer named Marsupia with a *very* unrealistic strength stat. I started raiding with Simon and his minotaur, Sketlios the Earth Mage, when I couldn't sleep and Jason snored away. Nina hardly ever logged on anymore, but she and I played *KrissKrossWords!* on our phones most days. Simon always hollered *For honor and King Minos!* into my damn headset when his minotaur charged some hapless gnome.

"I majored in Classics," he said apologetically over the headset. "Minotaurs are Greek, did you know?"

I did.

Life turned into one of Nina's bubbles of frozen time. The same day, repeating forever. Work, second work, home, eat, game, sleep.

"It's a little bit fascist, don't you think?" I said to Jason one night after he'd dragged himself home from a semi-successful round with some kind of plutonium elemental dude downtown. I couldn't help it. I was in the middle of some freshman's ethics midterm.

Jason looked up from his third bowl of Frosty Frogs, startled and hurt. "What the hell does that mean, Sam?"

"Well, *basically*, you're a cop without any of the things that hold cops back. Warrants, lawyers, Internal Affairs, the Fourth Amendment. You just . . . go out and beat on people less powerful than you." I typed, *The protection against unreasonable search and seizure is the core of the American justice system . . .*

"Bad people!"

I didn't look up from my laptop. *The Founding Fathers intended to protect all classes equally from the predatory nature of authoritarian government . . .* "Maybe. But it's not like you followed a chain of evidence to figure that out. It's not like you have to report to someone every time you use your power. You just seek and destroy and no one tells you no. It's like the Wild West, but you're the only ones with guns."

"Samantha, you don't know what you're talking about." MacArthur yowled at the change in our tone. Mommy and Daddy were fighting and it made his stomach hurt. "You're not out there with us; you don't see what the bad guys can do, what they *are*. You don't feel the . . . the *compulsion* of the Eidolons. They won't stand for us staying in and playing video games in our PJs. You can't comprehend the power they have. The power *we* have, the responsibility, the *stakes*. You're just . . ."

I gritted my teeth. "I'm just the only thing standing between us and the landlord. I'm just the only one of the two of us still living in the real world and not playing the world's most elaborate game of cowboys and Indians." *The Third Amendment prevents the quartering of soldiers in private homes without the consent of the owner . . .*

"That's not what I meant, baby." He touched the eagle on his button honking *The Wages of Sin Are Reaganomics* reflexively, reassuring himself. I wasn't sure which of us he was calling *baby*. "People love us . . ."

"People love you because you're magic, and face it, Jay: you used to be all about giving authority the middle finger. Now, you *are* Authority, with a capital A. You don't even paint for real anymore! All war, no art. And no Wall Street big shot has a tenth of the power you've got pinned to your fucking coat. You got a stencil for that?"

I shouldn't have said it. I wouldn't have, if I'd known that within a month, I'd be resting my head on a bag of kale while my vision slowly blurred and grew dark around the label on a tub of creamed honey. But I didn't know. Because Jason hadn't told me they'd moved on from pimply teenagers with super strength shaking down tourists. He wanted to protect me. Sad trombone. One time when we were juniors, Jason tagged the side of a posh day care center: an unvaccinated toddler playing with wooden blocks shaped like viruses—measles, whooping cough, smallpox—while his mother looked on in pride. Underneath, he'd written, IGNORANCE KILLS.

Doesn't it just.

A man came into Art Mart just before Halloween, which is basically Christmas for art supply stores. I had no reason to think a single thing of it. He looked like one of those dipshits who come to a gallery show and buy the most expensive piece just *because* it's the most expensive piece. He was the picture of a class war—early-middle-aged, fashionably bald, the kind of body you get from well-spoken steroids you can take home to Mother, dark suit, one of those peacocking shirt-and-tie combos: sapphire-blue button-down and a huge knot in his emerald paisley tie.

"Welcome to Art Mart, the one-stop shop for ghoulish bargains; how can I help you?"

The bald man looked me over. "Are you Samantha Dane?"

I blinked away a zombie haze of retail autopilot. "Yes?"

He snapped his fingers at me. "I know your work! *The Gallery System Is a Noose Around the Neck of the Artist*, right? I actually own *Boomer Fucks Love It When You Shoot Black and White*. It hangs right above my fireplace. What *happened* to you? So much promise."

"Boomer fucks love it when you fail," I quipped, as I have quipped many times before.

"Quite," Baldy laughed, but it seemed like he was laughing because that's what humans do when someone tells a joke, not because he thought I was particularly witty. He put one meaty mitt in his deep, dark pocket. "Well, Miss Dane, I'll confess I did not come to buy orange construction paper or spooky stencils. I heard through my friend Professor Yates that you worked here, and I was just *dying* to meet you. I administer an endowment for young artists, and every morning, I look at the fire in my hearth and see your work and wonder, *Damn, why doesn't powerful, outsider art like that ever get the chance it deserves while the same boring Yosemite landscapes get calendars and coffee mugs and place mats on every table?*"

I couldn't believe it was really happening. Daddy Warbucks

was gonna make me a star. We're in a movie now. Everything's A-OK. But then my stupid mouth, which is a more authentic artist than the rest of me, decided to vomit up some senior-project-mission-statement bullshit. "Well, I mean, probably because outsider art isn't about mass production . . ."

Mr. Business Q. Endowment waved his hand dismissively. "Of course, but mass production comes with the kind of money that buys *security*. Which, yes, my dear, boomer fucks also love. Because that kind of money makes problems just . . . poof! Blow away like leaves. Here." He gave me his card. "Come to my office tomorrow. You're perfect for the endowment. I'll have no trouble convincing the board."

"I can't tomorrow. It's my birthday," I mumbled weakly.

"The next day, then," said my new best friend. "Do we have a deal?"

He held out his hand. I took it, automatically. That's what humans do when someone in a suit sticks out his paw. I squeezed hard. My dad always told me even a girl should shake hands like a man. I want to say it felt strange, that it tingled or burned. But he just had dry, warm palms—and he didn't let go.

"When you see Jason," he whispered throatily, "tell him Reaganomics *saved* this country."

The businessman let go of my hand. I looked down at his thick, embossed card.

ISAAC AMENDOLARA

SECURITIES & FUTURES

"Happy birthday, Samantha Dane," Isaac said cheerfully, and left.

I never saw him again, even when he killed me.

• • •

Jason opened the door at 4:40 AM, bleary-eyed and bruised. I sat rigid on the couch, awake as a year of coffee, my veins screaming tension, and the second I saw his fingers around the doorjamb, I blurted out:

"Reaganomics *saved* this country!"

I burst into tears.

Jason knocked over the coffee table trying to get to me faster than a person can actually move. He kissed me, stroked my hair, and peered into my eyes like an ophthalmologist.

"Oh shit, oh shit, Sam, I'm so sorry. I didn't know he even *knew* about you. When did you see him? How long ago? Did he give you a business card? Where did he find you? What else did he say?"

I explained in sobs and gulps, fishing the card out of my pocket. Jason yanked it out of my hand, threw it in the sink, and lit the corner with a match, watching it stonily until it burned totally to ash.

"What the fuck? Jason, what the *shit*? I need that! He's going to give me a grant . . ."

Jason's jaw clenched. His face went hard and cold. "You know, the weird thing is he probably would. He's a man of his word." Jason sat down next to me. He fussed over me, touching my face, frantic, turbo-powered mothering and smothering. "That man you met today . . . he's like me. He has powers. He's after the Avant Garde and we're after him. He's a dealmaker. He offers you something, and when you shake on it, he tells you what he wants in return, which would be fine except you *have* to do it within twenty-four hours or the despair will make you pitch yourself out a window. He calls himself Six Figure."

I couldn't get my sweating under control. Jason brought me a new shirt. As I pulled it over my head, I whispered, "He looked like a lot more figures than that."

"I think he was just a middle-class guy when he started out. Now he runs the city, and he wants more. He's the real deal. Way beyond that freshman ethics essay you keep revising. Evil. Like Satan-in-the-Monsanto-building-in-whaleskin-boots evil. Did you tell him where we live?"

I shook my head. "I'm supposed to meet him, after my birthday. At his office. Jason, what about the card? You didn't have to *burn* it."

Jason grimaced. "Yeah, I did. It gives you cancer. If you hold on to it long enough. He's been handing them out all over town. I told you. Evil."

It was a long time till we slept. MacArthur kneaded the bedcovers and snored softly between us. Just as I was finally drifting off, Jason whispered:

"After your birthday, you should go visit my parents. I know they suck, but they live in Kentucky. Six Figure wouldn't be caught dead."

"Sure, darling," I sighed, and then I was eating white cheese and white wine in a gallery full of white hippos in Jacobean collars and I was asleep.

Hello, maraschino cherries.

Hello, farmer's-market tomatoes.

Hello, red and lovely things.

This is the last good thing I remember. I'm so cold. I can't feel my fingers or my toes. I want to remember this and nothing else.

I woke up to an envelope on Jason's pillow. Inside was a note:

All good Samanthas deserve birthday gifts

To find yours, my love, just get in the lift.

I pulled on pajama pants and a Blowhole T-shirt. I couldn't

wait. I ran out to the elevator. The doors opened—inside was a French impressionist paradise. Jason had painted *A Sunday Afternoon on the Island of La Grande Jatte* all around the walls of the elevator car. It was perfect. My favorite since I was a kid. The spray paint re-created the pointillism of the original better than I'd ever have thought.

And it was alive.

I stepped inside, shut the door, pulled the emergency stop. The alarm broke years earlier. Seurat's picnickers swirled around me, smiling, shaking my hand, bowing. The black dog and the little tan pug jumped up, leaving black and brown acrylic paw prints on my pajamas. The soldiers saluted and kissed both my cheeks. I couldn't stop crying and smiling and giggling. The sportsman flexed his arm for me and I clapped my hands. The ladies in their beautiful dresses gave curtseys. One held her black umbrella over my head, in case of rain. The monkey hooted noiselessly and ran up my leg onto my shoulder. And the handsome man in the top hat and suit bowed and held out his hand. I hesitated. I saw Six Figure's face in my mind, holding out his dry, warm hand.

No. It was my birthday. Fuck him.

The nobleman swept me into a waltz around the elevator, very cramped but very elegant. I swore I could hear the Seine lapping at the island shore. The man in the top hat kissed me, a real kiss, full of good wishes. His lips felt as smooth as a canvas.

They faded after an hour. I pulled the emergency stop out and rose back up toward my floor. My heart felt like a hot-air balloon. I couldn't stop smiling. I stepped out and practically skipped back to the apartment.

Simon stood in my kitchen, sobbing in black and white. He was holding MacArthur the Genius Cat. MacArthur was very dead.

Simon had twisted his pretty, silky striped neck horribly until it broke. I screamed. Simon screamed.

"I'm sorry!" he bawled. "I don't want to! It's not me! I don't want to do it!"

He pixelated into a minotaur. His minotaur. Sketlios the Earth Mage. The minotaur dropped my cat's corpse on the kitchen floor. I think I knew what was going to happen. I just couldn't believe it. It wasn't fair. I didn't do anything wrong. We're in a movie now. Everything's A-OK in the movies.

Simon beat me to death on my birthday with his monochrome minotaur fists, stripped me naked, and stuffed me in the refrigerator for Jason to find. He cried the whole time.

I love you, Marsupia.

For honor and King Minos.

We will avenge thee.

It's almost over. I was only barely alive when he crammed me in here. I tried to hold on. I tried really hard to not die.

Boomer fucks love it when you fail.

I guess my photographs will sell now. My hard drive is solid fucking gold the minute my breath stops.

I can't bear to think of Jason's face when he finds me. Us. Simon shoved MacArthur in the crisper drawer. I wish I could feel his fur. It would be comforting. But there's a sheet of glass between us. How will Jason ever be able to get over it? To forgive Simon? To unsee my blue fucking face smashed up against week-old pizza? But then I think—and it's almost the last thing I think—about that avenging thing. Because they will avenge me. I know it. I know it because we're in a movie now and I know how movies work. This is the second-act break. I'm an accepted part of the structure. Jason

Remarque will kill Six Figure because Six Figure killed me. It will be an amazing battle. Really fill the seats. And when it's over, he'll move on to bigger and better villains. He'll be the kind of famous I was gonna be. Eventually, he'll start dating again. Someone who understands the responsibility. The *stakes*. Though he'll probably never get another cat.

I try to cry out. One last effort to be not dead. My lips won't move.

I belong in the refrigerator. Because the truth is, I'm just food for a superhero. He'll eat up my death and get the energy he needs to become a legend.

Goodbye, broccoli.

Goodbye, grape juice, not from concentrate.

Goodbye, farm-fresh butter.

Goodbye, MacArthur the Genius Cat.

Goodbye, Nikon F1 camera with a red strap.

Goodbye, gallery system.

Goodbye, Jason.

THE HELL HATH CLUB VS. ETERNITY

Samantha Dane is almost melted enough to stand. We all help her up, even Pauline. Bayou drapes one of her arms over her shoulder. Daisy gets the other. Julia kisses the top of her head. Nobody says anything about her wearing nothing but a refrigerator. When they find her body, they'll put her in something nice and modest that has nothing to do with her and she'll wish she'd stayed like this.

It's all right. The dead don't do shame.

The Hell Hath Club walks its newest member out into the Lethe Café, into music and moonlight and steaming cups of nothing that taste like remembering. Her frozen blue skin gleams like the bottles behind the bar. We help her into the booth, hold her hand, slip her a joke or two to make her smile.

What's the difference between being dead and having a boyfriend?

Death sticks around.

She smiles. Samantha's smile is as strong as a superpower. Neil brings her a drink and waggles his claws shyly. When she lifts it to her chapped lips, there's a key in the cup, attached to a novelty skeleton keychain that says *Elysian Arms Apartment 14*.

"What do you know? You're just downstairs from me," I say. "The neighborhood's gone to hell, of course." I wink. She winks back.

Quarter Inch Bleed starts up a new song. The crowded dead roar joy. Gail steps up to the microphone, her tinsel-wrapped rhino horns proud and thick as horns of plenty, her long, sleek black fur gleaming like ink in the stage lights.

She starts to sing. By the time the chorus rolls around, we're all singing together, the infinite dead and the gargoyles and the evil clown and the scaly punk princess and the star-eater and the porn star and the science-queen of hypermercury and the girl in the refrigerator, giving no fucks for the hackneyed, predictable tales steaming on without us, full speed ahead. We escaped. The Deadtown moon turns all our faces into four-color saints, and for a moment, this moment, every night, we all feel almost alive again, dancing together at the end of the story, where nothing in heaven or earth can hurt us anymore forever.

ACKNOWLEDGMENTS

A book like *The Refrigerator Monologues* owes too many debts to count in the few small pages tucked in after the ending. It exists at the nexus of popular comics culture, and so takes inspiration from . . . nearly everything and everyone. One cannot thank the original authors of fairy tales when one retells them, but this is not the case when it comes to cape-and-caption tales. From the bottom of my heart, I would like to thank the pantheon of comics writers, artists, and creators—great and small—who built the grand superhero universe in which we all have been swimming in over the last century. None of my girls and none of my heroes could possibly exist without them, and even when I get my anger on, I have nothing but respect and honor for the monumental feat of deliberate mythology they have, and continue to, accomplish. Where I have thrown my BANG!s and POW!s, I have done it with love, and where I have dissected, I have, I hope, made as little mess in the lab as one could hope.

More specifically, the deepest bow and greatest thanks must go to Gail Simone, who first noticed, named, and collated evidence for the phenomenon of Women in Refrigerators and brought it to the attention of the culture at large and who has fought the good fight for decades. If there is any good in this work, some credit for it must go to her. On the other side of the coin, thank you to Eve Ensler, whose *The Vagina Monologues* detonated the theatrical scene when I was coming-of-age as a young feminist-actress type of thing. Both in title and structure, *The Vagina Monologues* gave me a sturdy framework on which to hang my frustration with the roles of women in superhero stories. This play was the first seed of *The Refrigerator Monologues*, the first thing that came to my mind in a Cuban bar on a rainy night in Baltimore, and it drove the car forever after.

Further gratitude must go to my editor, Joe Monti, who pursued this project and bolstered it almost from the moment it was concieved. No one could ask for a warmer, more personal, or more understanding editor, and no other editor's GIF game comes close. My agent, Howard Morhaim, continues to be the noble superhero sweeping in to rescue all my misbegotten children, and I would trust him till the ends of Metropolis and back.

Thank you to the coven: Leah, Rabbit, Kat, Shelle, Molly, Cylia, and Beth—friends so old that the word *friend* doesn't quite cut it anymore—who gave me such support and love that it would bring back the dead.

And thank you, finally and always, to Heath, my partner, who sat with me in that Cuban bar and tolerated me crying over a Spider-Man movie and never once said the idea of creating an entire superhero universe to make a point was ridiculous; who sat with me for weeks performing the Herculean task of brainstorming superhero and supervillain names that hadn't been used in the last hundred years; who gave me feedback and back rubs and backtalk and bacon sandwiches in equal measure. I love you right in the face.

STARRING:

Mary Jekyll, Diana Hyde, Catherine Moreau, Beatrice Rappaccini, and Justine Frankenstein!

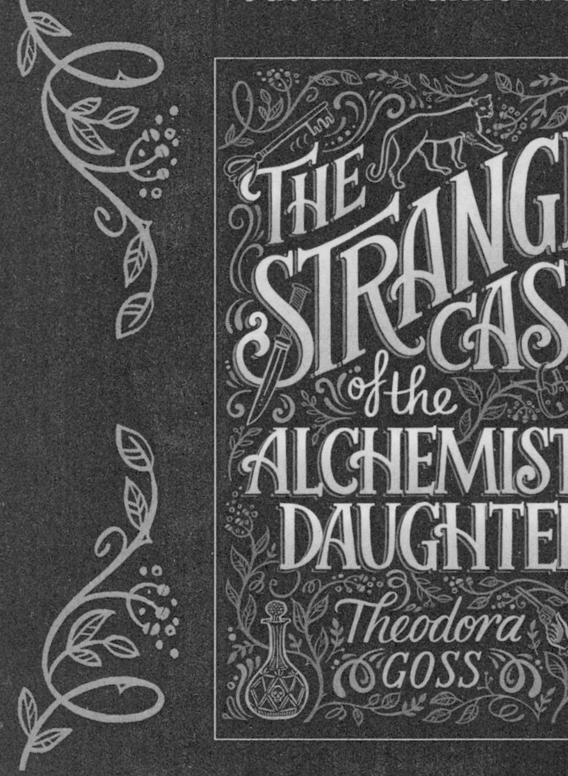

The daughters of literature's most famous mad scientists must come together to stop a murderer—and solve the mystery of their own creation.